DUE
DILIGENCE

SHAYNA GRISSOM

CONTENTS

I should've asked you questions

I should've asked you how to be

Asked you to write it down for me

Should've kept every grocery store receipt

'Cause every scrap of you would be taken from me

Watched as you signed your name Marjorie

All your closets of backlogged dreams

And how you left them all to me

What died didn't stay dead

What died didn't stay dead

You're alive, you're alive in my head

What died didn't stay dead

What died didn't stay dead

You're alive, so alive

And if I didn't know better

I'd think you were singing to me now

If I didn't know better

I'd think you were still around

I know better

But I still feel you all around

I know better

But you're still around

Marjorie by Taylor Swift

1

MARJORIE

The coffee steamed against the soppy chill of the morning. The morning always called to the familiar ache in her bones. Arthritis is an eventuality for anyone in their older years, but the diagnosis made things more official. Might as well include the AARP membership with the doctor's orders to use a fiber supplement. Having the diagnosis for arthritis next to the bottle of aspirin meant senior citizenship was official.

I can't be old. Kim isn't ready yet. That was precisely why she wanted to have all her children at a young age. She succeeded in doing just that with Gail and Steven. Only the third took his time and left so much broken. By the time Marjorie was physically able to have another, ten years had passed, and her heart felt as though it were on the other side of the umbilical cord.

The doctor said having another baby would help. When would she learn to stop listening to men? She supposed it didn't make much of a difference now.

"John," Marjorie called. "Coffee's hot."

The floors in the bedroom creaked and the door opened. Her husband emerged from the bedroom with his shuffling gait. Spinal surgery did a number on that man. His vertebrae fused along the lower sections; he never regained agility from the knees down. Just as well, it was time to hang up the hat anyhow.

She served him coffee at the head of the table with a raspberry jam-filled scone. He chewed it with his bare gums, not ready to put his dentures in so early in the morning.

"Did Kim make her car payment?"

Marjorie's face tensed. When she didn't answer, he nodded and took another sip of coffee. He must have seen the bank statements. She needed to find a better place to hide them. For a man who could barely read or write, he was quick with numbers. His expression placid... John wasn't upset that she made the car payment.

"I didn't want it to reflect badly on her."

"This one is a dud too."

Same old story. Kim would come waltzing in with a new boyfriend. He'd be presented like a promise. Full of potential and earnestness to take care of their little girl. After a few months—or sometimes weeks—they'd learn otherwise.

"Young men aren't what they used to be," Marjorie complained.

"She's a beautiful girl. She could find herself a doctor or a lawyer..."

The Navy brat had his hooks in their daughter in a way she'd never seen before. Kim was working two jobs and still borrowing money from them. She'd go out with that boy and come back sobbing several days later.

"She's going to break up with him," Marjorie said. "She told me so last week."

One good thing about Kim was that she always bounced back, no matter how hard the breakup. John didn't need all the details. He had enough on his plate, and bruises on their daughter's body would only send his blood pressure surging through blocked arteries the cholesterol medicine couldn't seem to control.

There was also no sense in telling him that Kim might be pregnant. *What's done is done.*

Maybe a child would be good for Kim. A baby would have to take priority over the string of deadbeats she brought home. Why that girl was so adamant about being in a relationship was beyond Marjorie. You'd think that if a girl learned anything in this house, it was that men couldn't be depended on.

A chill rattled her then. Maybe that was the lesson Kim learned.

The thud of a car door slammed from outside. Not just once, but twice.

Leaning back, Marjorie peered out the window and saw the yellow sedan in the driveway. Dread took hold where the coffee should've been, and the left side of her face began to twitch.

Marjorie loved her daughter — all her children — with every aching bone in her body. They had grown up to be wonderful people. She'd do anything for them, no matter the cost, but Kim never stopped costing. Sometimes Marjorie feared their youngest daughter would take everything. Swallow the world whole and still need more. It wasn't fair to Gail and Steven, she knew that, but what else could she do?

"Looks like she brought company," John said.

The tall figure looming over their daughter suggested she brought Marv, or rather, he brought her. Driving her car that they were making payments on because he took all of Kim's wages to do God knew what. The left side of her face got hot and prickly all over. It happened sometimes when stress overwhelmed her. Just another feature of getting old, she guessed.

Kim walked in and muttered a greeting, but her eyes couldn't meet Marjorie's. A low, seething tremor took hold. Why couldn't her daughter look at her?

"What's wrong?"

About that time, Gail came down the stairs. Her long hair ironed straight, and the smell of her rich perfume unfurled throughout the house. Marjorie's Chanel girl. A single bottle of perfume cost more than a week's worth of groceries.

"What's with you?" Gail asked, stopping short of Kim and her boyfriend.

"I'm moving out," Kim said. "I'm just grabbing a few things."

Marjorie tensed on uncertain legs. That wasn't the plan. Kim was going to break up with the stoney faced man with the strong hands and wicked temper. She was going to have the baby here and they would all raise it together.

"Kim..." Marjorie moved in to scoop up her baby, but Kim shoved her away and ran upstairs. The rejection sent her world rocking. Her Kim never pushed her away. Even when grounded before prom, her daughter never turned down a hug.

Marv's massive hands flexed but he remained fixed in front of the door as the walls came closing in on Marjorie. Where did she go wrong?

Turning to John, Marjorie implored him to do something. *Say something. You don't know what kind of trouble he's going to get her in. What he's already gotten her in to!* Marjorie spared him from the worst details but that backfired on her as John shrugged.

"She needs to learn how to fend for herself, Marg."

Turning to Gail, Marjorie caught the rage in her daughter's eyes. She knew. The girls were always close despite their age. Gail and Jacob moved back in to save money for a house after college and thank God for that.

Gail stared down the tall, pale man and snarled before rushing upstairs after Kim. Marjorie never did understand the inner workings of Gail's mind. However, she did learn to trust her daughter. Gail's fiery responses sometimes clashed with her icy demeanor, but all with good reason.

Marv lurched like he was about to follow but that's when John stood. "The girl's room is off limits," her husband said.

Standing between him and the stairway, Marjorie had no time to decide what came next. Not recalling exactly when she left the kitchen. Perspiration pasted to her nightgown. John stood to get the measure of the man before him. Towering nearly two feet over him, John caught the gravity of the situation. Marv's hollow eyes, soulless and bleak, flickered toward the ceiling as if he were a predator gauging his prey's whereabouts. The car keys stowed in his pocket.

"I think you should leave," John said.

As if the words were a dare, Marv started walking right past her. She stepped in front of him, but he was quick on those long legs of his and simply evaded her and rushed up the stairs. The sheer boldness of it had Marjorie staggering. What kind of person just ignores people in their own home?

"I'm calling the police!" Marjorie rushed to the phone mounted on the wall.

Spinning the dial on the phone, she reached emergency services.

"Police? We have a trespasser; he's refusing to leave. I think he means to hurt my girls."

What the operator said didn't matter. The pounding in her heart got so loud. Shouts reverberated from upstairs. Her girls were in danger. Her husband tried to pull his useless legs up the stairs. The left side of her face buzzed as her vision pirouetted. The splintering of frames confirmed it. Slamming against the bedroom door over and over.

"Go away!" Gail's voice was shrill. Maybe they'd use the fire escape as they often did to sneak out for farm parties. The bonfire gatherings Marjorie often caught glimpses of in the lower lands. Her daughters never went where she couldn't reach them, but this time might be different.

Marjorie rattled off the address. "Please come. He's trying to break into the girl's bedroom."

"I'm getting my gun!" John yelled.

They both knew he didn't have one. The butcher took the older cows past their prime and the vet euthanized any pets. John hated seeing anything in pain. He'd be up all night if an animal got sick. His blood pressure would skyrocket and he'd pace the night away. A gun just didn't make sense when he couldn't pull the trigger.

But Marv didn't know that. Maybe it would be enough to scare the man. Send him running. She paused half a dozen heartbeats, but the banging persisted. What kind of man didn't fear being shot? She heard rumors about Marv. That he ran with the bikers and collected debts. Kim said he had a rough childhood and wanted out of that life. He just needed her love and support. Marjorie always believed her for some stupid reason.

"Get the fuck off my property!" John shouted. "The police are on their way."

The very foundation of the house bowed under the strain of Marv's fierce blows. Solid wood painstakingly framed and selected on the verge of being smashed to bits. She had to do something. John couldn't make it up those stairs. Even if he could, he'd be powerless against that monstrosity. He was a strong man, her husband, but without balance. If his swollen knuckles got a hit, it would be over, but Marv was too quick.

Not her girls. Not under her roof.

2

HOMECOMING

I t was a need I couldn't rationalize.

Like a flight of birds determined to navigate thousands of miles on instinct alone or a phantom limb that aches before a heavy rain. The rational mind can think circles around instinct, but instinct will always win. It wasn't my home anymore. My family departed this forlorn property years ago, yet here I was.

No reason for me to come back, but my eyes always sought the house on the hill like a compass pointing north. Instinct drove me here. As if all of life's problems would vanish if I returned. A gut feeling I'd rather not have.

Ask me about my favorite birthday or to describe the face of my best friend as a child and I couldn't tell you. I couldn't recall yesterday's breakfast, but I remembered my grandparents' house. Right down to the small brick-colored tiles in the kitchen. The dried drippings of black paint on the support beam I once treated like a fireman's pole.

A sliding glass door with jagged chunks of old glass from a time well before I was born. I knew how it broke, but I made Grandma tell me the story over and over just to hear her laugh. Her only son tried to run through it, shattering one of the panes.

Nineteen steps to the second story.

The room my aunt and mother kept had access to a space between the walls. In the back of the closet, they kept their treasures behind a plank of wood nailed to the wall. A secret my mother showed me the time we trespassed.

Steady feet must always remain on the support beams, otherwise I'd fall through the ceiling and land on Grandpa's mustard corduroy chair where he watched TV and chewed on an endless supply of homemade beef jerky. A habit to replace the two packs a day— again, before I was born.

The living room had carpet. A brown, shaggy affair worn into patch nubs where I sat and played with the blocks Grandpa carved and painted just for me. Something about toys from China having lead-based paint. The earpiece clipped to one ear relayed the news reports he watched constantly while Grandma did everything that needed doing.

I had only lived there a short time. After Grandpa died, Grandma sold the farm. I was seven. Trying to recall my time there was like looking out a foggy window, but I still craved it. Clinging to what little I had left like a security blanket. Always searching for that feeling again. Childhood. Nowhere was safer or nearly as idyllic as the farmhouse on the hill. Its great bay windows created a picture-perfect view of Mount Rainier. Whenever it stormed, the windows rattled, but they were supposed to, or at least that's what I was told. Better to bend than break.

Parked across the street of my childhood home, I leaned against my Outback and finished the Winston cigarette while I scowled at the brown picket fence.

"They painted it brown," I said.

My husband, with his hands in the pockets of his slacks, nodded apologetically. "It's their home now. They can paint it however they want."

"Grandpa and I whitewashed the fence before he died. He only put it up so I wouldn't fall into the creek."

Christian's eyes narrowed at the hill just below the fence. "I don't see a creek."

"It's there. The grass on that hill overgrows and it's too steep to use a riding lawnmower."

He nodded. "So, he put up the fence."

I ground my cigarette with the bottom of my boot like it didn't pay up. Why did I come back here? This was a stupid idea. "We used to fish in it."

"Catch anything?"

I shook my head. No. There were no fish in the creek. Just a small,bored child needing something to do. It must have been comical for people driving by. They would just assume we were fishing in the tall, lush grass. The only giveaway was the cattails swaying in the country air. And by country air, I mean it reeked of cow manure. An earthy, ripe smell. Pungent like freshly cut grass, but digested through four stomachs. Some farmer scooped it up and sprayed it across acres of fields.

We leaned against the car together and watched as families with small children flocked through the gravel driveway. Some held their parents' hands or clung to their sides, others had to be carried. It must have been tiring. Lugging around twenty pounds of belligerence smeared in sticky fruit-flavored snacks.

Kids are cute. I just never felt the need to have them. I took classes in college on childcare just in case I changed my mind like everyone said I would. If I learned anything from those classes, it was that I was woefully unprepared. Kids need so much. What if I didn't have enough?

"You want to go in?" Christian asked.

My stomach flipped.

More than anything. I wanted to go inside and see the world so ingrained in my memory. To reconfirm the cow trough was not, in fact, a pool. A tiny, amused smile worked across my face. I was furious with grandma over that trough. Not because I was told no, but because I thought she was trying to trick me the way so many grown-ups trick children to avoid inconvenience.

In the backdrop, the silo peeked above the trees, its tin roof rusting and falling away. The new owners couldn't tear it down after it became a nesting place for endangered owls.

"Don't want to make it weird. It's their home now. Not mine."

"We don't have to tell them anything."

No, we didn't, but the rims of my eyes were already hot and threatening to tear up. Nothing like an unhinged woman crying in the middle of a pumpkin patch. Maybe I'd find a dark corner of the hay maze and cry it out. Or go behind the shed if it became too much. How to even explain it without sounding unhinged?

My grandparents raised their children there. My childhood ended the day we drove away. Their history somehow blurred into my own, creating an emotional attachment to things I'd never seen for myself.

"I'm sure they'd understand," Christian said.

I closed my eyes and took in the warmth of his hand as it rubbed my back. "You have some wonderful memories here. I bet they'd love to hear it."

He always knew the right thing to say. I was going to offer the new owners confirmation that they bought the right home. An offer, not an ask.

"Okay, but I won't press the issue. If they don't invite us in, un-prompted, we leave it at that."

"That's fine," he laughed.

Of course he wouldn't press the issue. Christian had a natural charisma that opened the doors I never could. Maybe if I saw the farm for what it is now and not what my mind piecemealed together, I'd be able to gain some closure. Maybe my heart would find new earth to take root in.

The kids in their little rubber rain boots and matching rain jackets skipped in puddles and bounced in place. Their little faces lit up with the promise of pumpkins and games. It was so wholesome. So perfect.

All around us stood multi-million-dollar homes with energy efficient windows glaring at the eyesore on the best lot for miles. It must have wrecked the neighbor's property value.

But the world needed more pumpkin patches. I couldn't keep this place going. This might have been the best use for it. Five and a half acres devoted to filling the hearts of children and healthy animals.

I could live with that.

The new owners converted the pony stall into a goat pen. A far better use of the space. Kids were climbing on the bars to feed springy pygmy goats wearing pumpkin pajamas.

Families laughed as the tiny goats jumped off their wooden boxes and slid down the slides on their butts. Wrapping my cardigan tighter against the damp chill, I noted the makeshift coffee stand that gave out hot cider fresh from the farm's orchard.

A little pang of indignation struck me then. My grandparents planted most of those apple trees. Grandma would shoo away the peacocks and pick apples for me. They were retired by then, so most of the apples went to the deer every morning.

I shrugged off the envy, reminding myself that I'm no farmer. It's not a skill set bequeathed to me at birth. I'd never milked a cow. All those apples would go to waste under my watch.

Stacked hay bales with pumpkins for family photos and in the lower fields were speckled with orange blobs and wheelbarrows. Farmhands and volunteers were everywhere, still bringing in pumpkins and squash since apple season had fully withered.

"Holy shit," Christian said. "I'm exhausted just watching them."

"It takes a lot of work to run a farm."

Not that I had any firsthand experience. Just stories. "We used to hire a third of the local tribe as farmhands just to get the dairy processed."

We...no. That was a lie. I did none of that. I wasn't even born yet when the farmhands came to the house for breakfast and lunch. My grandparents and I lived alone. We didn't have a single chicken. In the twilight of their years, it was all they could do to keep their tired, broken bodies moving for my sake.

Though we had a pet racoon. Grandpa rescued it after someone ran over his mother. Rocky the Racoon wasn't the most affectionate pet a child could have. He skittered around on the tiles with long, sharp claws and Grandpa put him in the pen outside the front door when I played in the living room. Not trusting the wild animal with the only grandchild stateside.

"Not me," I clarified. "My grandparents."

If Christian heard that last part, he ignored it as if it were really my experience all along when we all knew otherwise.

The supports for the porch were thick metal beams, just as I remembered. Four feet apart, and they served as posts for the railing. A concrete porch is easy to hose off and was wide enough for several picnic tables, now stacked with hay bales and pumpkins. A plastic table served as a blockade to the front door. The new owners were on the other end of the table, checking out customers with pumpkins and jugs of cider, and stamping hands for rides on the tractor. One glimpse at the sandwich board and I was relieved to see the bulk of the pricing was under five dollars.

Ingenious really. The perfect setup for the purchase of pumpkins and jugs of cider. Entry to the farm was free as were the corn maze and corn pit where small children buried themselves in dried kernels.

A few dollars here, a few dollars there. Not a single thing cost more than a latte yet almost everyone in line had a jug or pumpkin. They were using a microtransaction technique. The distracted teenage boy in the discolored lawn chair scrolled through his phone while a rough-cut man with dark shaggy hair hassled him.

"You think you can hand me some bags?"

The boy rolled his eyes at the imposition. Some things never change. Farm kids never want to be on the farm. It's those of us who live in the concrete jungles who want to be here.

Two girls around five and eight with matching ribbons in their braided pigtails came swooping to their father's rescue with brown paper sacks with twine handles. The farmer smiled at them. "Thanks, sweeties."

Right on cue, Christian moved toward them. I reached for his arm to try and stop him, but he was already alongside the plastic table introducing himself to the owner. Couldn't we just be invisible for a little while longer? What if they didn't want us there and asked us to leave?

I hung back and watched them exchange handshakes and pleasantries while my stomach dipped to a new low.

There were more words before the farmer locked eyes on me. When Christian pointed in my direction even the autumn wind couldn't stop the heat rising along my neck.

"Paul," the farmer said. "Take over, will you?"

He was tall but the beginnings of a hunch formed along his neck. Oh, I didn't want to be a nuisance. The line lengthened and the teen, Paul, grimaced at his newly assigned task. Nothing worse than inconveniencing a small business at what was probably the busiest time of the year.

"Hi, I'm Robert Miles. Your husband said you grew up here."

I laughed nervously and clutched Christian's arm. "I'm so sorry, I didn't mean to intrude—"

"No," he said. His dark brown eyes and hair gave an indigenous look. Maybe he's from the tribe. That would be glorious. Nothing would make the white wealth in this area shudder like a Native owning the property they couldn't. This land sat on the threshold of the reservation, so it would've made sense.

"I'm really happy to meet you. We didn't get a lot of information when we bought the place. I'd love to know the history."

Okay, so not a local. It was a small town. Someone should have told him something. Had everyone forgotten about one of the largest dairy farms this side of Washington state? What was once a massive farm that sprawled over thirty acres produced enough dairy to keep every fridge stocked this side of the cascades. I smiled despite the confusion. Maybe the cutbacks involved the local museum.

Thirty years of service to a community, so quickly forgotten. A notion far more abrasive than the bales of dry, golden hay.

"You're not from here?" I asked.

"No, I'm from Colorado. Come in," he waved his hand toward the door. "We can talk inside where it's warmer."

I glanced up at Christian who was nodding. Robert Miles wanted to know about the house, and I wanted to see the house. A fair exchange. I just hoped someone would come and relieve his son of his duties before too long.

Following Robert into the house through the second front entrance I paused to gauge the overcast sky. Heavy, slate clouds were hanging low, and the air smelled wet. Any minute now and a torrential downpour would empty out the pumpkin patch anyway.

"So, maybe you can explain the two front doors," Robert said as we walked down the center hallway of the house. Lined with concrete and white floor to ceiling cabinets on one side. Easy to hose down after a dozen workers changed out of their mud-covered boots and raincoats.

"The garage was converted into a rec room," I said. "So, they created a covered mudroom for the workers."

Robert raised his brows as if impressed. "That explains a lot. We bought it sight unseen, so we had no context."

"This used to be a dairy farm, so after work, everyone would come in and trade their rubber boots and jackets here."

We gazed down the long galley of concrete floors and painted white cupboards. The sliding glass door that my uncle broke still stood after all these years. Because it was twice the size of a standard sliding glass door, it was cheaper to put new glass in. Why the workers left the existing broken glass inside, I never knew.

"Your parents built the house?"

"My grandparents, yeah."

"I'm really glad you came," Robert said. "Truth be told, we bought this farm at auction. Only way we could've afforded it."

I nodded. Grandma mentioned it. With no end to the recession in sight, it was all I could do to hang on to the job I had. Auctions were cash-only affairs, and we were just now coming to a place of financial stability. Not enough to have substantial savings, but we could pay the bills and Christian's business was finally taking off. He put in his two weeks at his day job, soon we'd be relying on his building expertise to pay the bills full-time.

"It's been rough," I agreed.

"Yeah, that's why we don't charge admittance for the pumpkin patch," Robert said, turning to the left to open the door to the house proper. "Kids need something to look forward to."

He was a good man. I could feel it. Earthy and honest. Robert would never be the man who made beautiful speeches at weddings or interpret the nuance in art, but his compassion was as defined as the callouses on his hands.

"Amy," he called as the three of us veered left into the kitchen.

My fingers traced the wall where the swinging doors once hung. A full-figured woman with a head full of blond hair was wrapped up in a messy bun at the top of her head. She wore black leggings with paint stains and a thick linen apron while she stood at the stove beside a large pot.

In a moment, I was transported back to childhood where Grandma prepped beef jerky. The entire kitchen almost-island, (peninsula, maybe?) would be covered in paper towels that soaked up the extra marinade while the dehydrators hummed. She made so much of the stuff. Grandpa chewed on it to stave off smoking and other snacking habits.

"This is Mindy," Robert explained to Amy. "Her family built the house."

The way her face brightened the moment he explained set me on my heels. Just the eagerness of it. My eyes shifted to Christian. He didn't meet my eyes, that would be rude, but there was a tenseness in his posture that suggested he noticed it too.

"Oh, we have so many questions!" Amy said.

So did I.

Like why no one else was willing or able to give them answers. The recession might have been a lot harder on the farming towns than they were in Seattle. On the outside it didn't seem to be the case maybe, but the property had exchanged hands several times over the years. This was the first family to stay longer than six months.

"Come and join us at the table, can I get you some coffee? Cider?" Robert was probably teasing, but I wanted the cider.

"If you have some inside, I'd love it. My grandparents planted those apple trees."

Passing the peninsula, I stopped short of the dining room and gasped.

The long, oval dining table with the matching chairs... He used Hemlock and while the finish had dulled some, I'd know it anywhere.

"What's wrong?" Christian asked, pulling me in tight.

"That's our table," I said. "Grandpa made it, chairs and all."

The Miles couple overheard what I'd said and joined us. "Your grandfather made this? That's amazing," Robert said. "It came with the house. Did you not know?"

A grainy lump bobbed in my throat.

I didn't know.

When Grandpa died, Grandma's departure from the farm was swift and she moved into a small apartment in town. It made sense that she'd sell it with the house. It seated eight people comfortably and twelve if there was a party. It wouldn't fit in a senior home.

"I guess no one wanted it."

Robert sat at the head of the table nearest the front door. That was Grandpa's chair— no, not anymore. Grandpa had died twenty years ago on my birthday. Neither Gail nor Steven deemed it necessary to take it, so here it remained.

It didn't stop me from sitting to his right though. That was where I always sat before. Even when that chair was set aside for the highchair, that was my place. Amy sat to the left of Robert, not at all aware of the symbolism. Not even Christian would understand, but maybe the house would.

Cupping my hot cider, it smelled like cinnamon and a melody of the sweet apples that grew in the orchard, but there was something else.

A note mold or something rotten.

The flecks in the cup were nothing more than ground spices. Something wasn't right, but what? I couldn't explain it. Everyone sipped the hot cider and spoke about how delightful it was, but once I picked up the smell of mildew, it was all I could taste. Filling my sinuses. My throat struggled to swallow the impending threat.

"We'd love to hear about your grandparents," Robert said.

Amy was nodding. "Any information about the house would be super helpful."

What was the issue? It was pasteurized. Helpful information about what? I saw Amy cooking it with the thermometer clipped to the pot. The house had indoor plumbing now, but that wasn't helpful, was it? Even if something was wrong with the apples, it didn't make it out of the pasteurization process.

The smell remained and I didn't know what was helpful.

I was home, wasn't I? This was what I wanted. To see the house and form a connection to the new owners to ease my mind. Even if I couldn't afford the property or maintain the farm, it was nice to know it was in good hands.

So why did I get the feeling that something was terribly wrong?

3

— · —

THICKENED

The rain came down in a torrential onslaught. It pelted with great thwacks against the roof. The flimsy gold painted rods that supported white lace curtains on the front windows were gone, revealing the chaos outside. Patrons were fleeing with their hoods drawn low over their faces. Some, like me, made the mistake of not wearing rainproof jackets.

"Oh..." I said as everyone turned to behold the spectacle.

"We got you covered," Robert said, kicking an old milk can repurposed as an umbrella stand. The aluminum tank echoed, prompting an unwanted flinch.

Mounts Family Dairy was hammered into the side. They must have found one of the old milk cans lying around. Robert had no idea he just kicked what most of my family members kept as mementos from their life here. Those cans were costly for my grandparents to make, and he just kicked it like a piece of junk.

I refocused on my cup. It's a metal canister, already covered in rust. The family could've thrown them out, but they chose to keep them and make them useful. Didn't that count for something?

"I can bring the car up," Christian said.

"It doesn't rain as much here as everyone ranted about," Robert said. "I lived in Alabama for twelve years—that was rain."

"How long have you guys lived here?" I asked, slowly spinning the ceramic mug with my fingertips.

"We moved in last March," Amy said. "A lot of this stuff was still left over from the last owners. Whoever they were, they left in a hurry."

Robert shrugged. "We needed all the help we could get."

"Who leaves a new tractor?" Amy said.

The strain in her voice signaled a warning. A motivation—something serious on their minds and they didn't know how to talk about it. Worry ignited from Amy to me. A new tractor cost a lot of money. No one would just leave one.

"Hard times," Robert said. "Maybe they moved across state and didn't have time to sell it."

My eyes flipped between Robert and Amy. She barely blinked, and her jaw sat tense. Something was going on between them and the last thing I wanted to do was get involved. We had just met these people, getting involved in their marital issues was not on my afternoon agenda. I turned to Christian. *Please say something. Make it less weird.*

"So, Mindy's grandparents built the house in the fifties?" he prompted.

"Yeah," I eagerly took the prompt. "They built it from scratch and put the indoor plumbing in later. Back in the day, this farm spanned down the hill and around the road. They had Jersey cows."

"Most of the properties out here are still on septic, right?" Robert asked.

I nodded and saw Amy shift a little in her chair. "We've been having issues with the septic. If there's a clog, the plumbers can't find it and say the septic is empty, but the backups are disturbing."

"It could be just rusty—" Robert said but was interrupted by the two brunette girls with braided pigtails.

"And these are our daughters," he introduced. "Charity and Lacy."

Both girls turned to smile politely at the strangers in their home but were quick to get to what they wanted. "Paul said we can't go into the orchards by ourselves."

"And Paul is right." Amy said. "It's a giant mud puddle."

The girls broke into protests at once. A little grin crept across my face as they assured their parents they wouldn't splash in the mud. They would stay clean. No accidents and lots of promises. All the adults at the table knew the truth. The moment those two girls went tromping down that hill, one would go mud sliding and the other would follow.

If they were already dirty, what did it matter if they came back as mud monsters? That was the whole point of the mudroom. They could change their clothes and walk through the hallway into the house's single bathroom. Even our dinky apartment had two bathrooms. I couldn't imagine making do with one.

Talking over the girls, Amy made her point known to us as well as the girls. "We don't want another repeat shower incident."

I tensed as Charity and Lacy blanched. They were practically trembling. A septic backup wasn't pretty by any means. Little could be worse than a tub filling with raw sewage, but the girls' fear tugged at my already fraying nerves.

"What happened with the tub?" I asked.

Robert embraced the girls with a hug before whispering to them to go upstairs. The lively, bouncy little became sullen and nodded. They didn't say another word. After being reminded of the bathtub, they lost all enthusiasm. It was deeply unsettling for me. Even though I didn't have kids, I still felt the urge to protect them. Christian gnawed at the inside of his cheek. He only did that when something upset him.

After several moments, Amy took her husband's hand and began their story.

"Charity was in the shower when it happened. She started screaming. Robert was running errands and the door was locked so Paul had to break it down. We found her in the shower covered in what looked like blood."

I stopped spinning my mug. Rust is a common issue in old houses, but that would've been common anywhere. The water would be a brownish red for a few minutes and stop.

"Like... thick and dark red?" Christian confirmed, just to make sure we were all on the same page.

Amy nodded. "It wasn't just a septic backup; it was coming from the shower itself. My poor baby was covered in it. It was hot and smelled like blood."

"I called the plumber as soon as I got home," Robert said. "They couldn't find anything wrong with the well or the septic."

I didn't know what to think.

Sitting back in the chair my grandfather made, I racked my brain for any logical reason for this. Part of me wanted to be angry at them. How dare they suggest the happiest place in my life was their nightmare. But that wasn't their intent. Their poor girls were terrified by something adults couldn't explain and they were only looking for answers.

"You saw it too?" I asked Robert.

"It drained by the time I got home, but the grout is still stained from it."

Suddenly, I got Amy's indirect tensions. Robert was skeptical of an experience very real to her and the children. What would I do if Christian didn't believe me? Given my family history, he would have a right to do so, but oh would it sting. Sorrow wrapped in mistrust, tied with a gold band with a vow on top. We'd never be the same again.

I didn't want them to be afraid in the house.

I'm sorry Christian, but I'm putting you to work...

I looked to my husband and there wasn't a shred of hesitation. God, I loved him.

"It just so happens I own a business building homes," he said. "I'd be happy to look into this for you."

Slipping my hand to his thigh, I gave it a squeeze. In an instant Amy's eyes welled and a single sob hitched in her throat. "You'd really do that for us?"

"We can't afford it," Robert said. "If you see something, you can just tell me how to fix it."

"As it happens," Christian said, taking the conversation in a direction I didn't expect but should have. "I'm looking to hire someone to help me on jobs. I can train you up, help you get any certs you need. Think of this as on-the-job training. Your son could work with us too sometimes."

He wanted to hire someone now that his business had become a full-time job. The plan was to have me working as his project manager once he got enough jobs lined up. Hiring Robert would mean I'd need to work at my current job a little longer, but given the situation, I didn't mind.

He was so good. Too good to be real. I gave his thigh a second squeeze higher up. A promise of what would come tonight. A glimmer of mischief in his blue eyes. Message received.

"I don't know what to say," Robert said.

Christian turned his head towards the window. "Well, not much we can do now. Once the rain lets up, we can do some inspecting."

He took one of the umbrellas out of the dairy tank and got the car while I set to work exchanging our phone numbers. This wasn't exactly charity. Christian was a businessman after all. Truth be told, we needed a portfolio if we were going to convince people that his business could handle custom builds.

All he had lined up currently were renovations on apartment complexes. Good money and corporations that always paid on time, but it didn't exactly dazzle. While this house had seen better days, the average property around here ran well into the millions. If Christian worked his magic on this house, all those wealthy neighbors would take notice.

It was a leap, starting a home building company in the middle of a recession. One that led to conversations well into the morning and more than one fight. But if there was one person worth trusting, it was Christian.

Amy and Robert followed me out and stopped short of the porch. Paul had abandoned his post and returned to the chair. Bundled up in a tan coat, his back was towards us while on the phone, not at all interested in the strange couple in his home.

"We'll call you and get something scheduled," I promised.

Back on the main road, Christian finally spoke. "What do you make of that story?"

"About the blood in the bathtub?" I asked. Between the damp and the defrost setting, my skin chilled and trembled. "I don't know. I don't think she was lying, but what could possibly explain that?"

Eyes on the road, Christian frowned. His dark thick brows knitted across his forehead. "Look at this neighborhood, Mindy."

What was once farmland and rustic little ranches were now extravagant homes. People stabled their horses here after the occasional ride. Luxury cars parked in the driveways. Adult toys like boats and RVs were carefully stowed in custom built garages.

It was hard to believe that places like this existed less than a mile away from people living in their cars and showering at the YMCA. When crippling poverty and exorbitant luxury were neighbors, it left little room for people like us. I didn't envy the wealthy. They could be as well off as they want, good for them. I only coveted the security money provided. Of not having to ration resources and hope nothing broke down in the process.

My thoughts were on the business when it came to the community, but Christian saw something else. Something only a home builder would recognize. He knew just how far people would go to get what they wanted.

"You think someone is sabotaging them?"

"A single dumpy house can drop the value of a community. The recession already has most of these homes underwater. I think someone wants the property and is trying to drive the price down."

I pressed my back into the seat. No one wanted that property more than me, but to terrorize the family that way only fueled my desire to help them stay. The worst possible outcome would be for my grandparents' farm to turn into some commercial property or a summer residence for a rich tool.

"How would they do it though?" I asked.

Christian's eyes flickered to my face for a moment, but he kept a steady eye on the road, always careful when I was in the car. "Remember that gel we got at the sex store that one time?"

A smile grew wide across my face. I knew exactly what he was referring to. It was some kind of powder that turned the bath water to a blue gel. Afterwards, running water broke it down and it slipped harmlessly down the drain.

"You think they used something like that?"

"I don't know how, but I'm willing to bet someone is sabotaging the property."

Based on the track record of buyers who promptly moved, I had to agree. Each time the property became cheaper and cheaper until foreclosed and at auction. One more time and the place would be cheap enough for even us to buy.

"They're nice people," I said. "They don't deserve that."

"Agreed."

We drove down the long stretch of road to return to the highway. The greenest grass grew on both sides of the road as it stretched toward the mountain. Totally unchanged despite twenty years. Still, what kind of neighbor would do that to a poor family? They did free pumpkin patches and made their living off selling apples and cider.

Maybe this place was unchanged on the outside, but behind closed gates and fancy stone siding, something had gone sour.

4

— · —

FIXER UPPER

Christian had some work to do in his office, so I kicked back on the sofa with a glass of red and called my aunt to tell her about the day.

"Hey," Gail said.

"You're not going to guess where I was today."

"... The farm?"

My enthusiasm utterly deflated. I wished she was Grandma. If she was, she'd play along with the conversation even though she already knew exactly what I was up to. Gail didn't indulge anyone, especially not those she deemed as fools.

"I met the new owners," I said. Desperate to move the conversation forward. "They're such good people. They have a free pumpkin patch for the kids."

"Oh, how sweet," she said.

How could she care so little? Gail grew up there. Like my mother, she took her kids there to be babysat. Every birthday. Every Christmas and Thanksgiving was held at that house. The massive Christmas tree was overburdened by school-made ornaments that Grandma carefully wrapped in newspaper for the following year.

I just didn't understand. How could her mother, my grandmother, put so much love and effort into our lives just for Gail and Steven to shrug it off?

"You should go see it," I said. "The house is mostly the same as we left it."

Gail groaned at that. "Does it still have that broken down silo?"

"That serves as nesting grounds for an endangered species?" I reminded her. "Yeah, it's still there."

"One strong breeze is all it would take..."

I rubbed the space between my brows. If it were Grandma on the phone, she'd be so happy. She'd tell me stories and she'd be happy to hear that three children now run around the property. There should always be children in that house.

"It has its problems," I agreed. "Christian and I are going to help them fix it up. Just a little pro-bono work."

"That's nice, but Christian needs to focus on his company. Now's not the time to give free labor away. Especially not on a lost cause."

"It's our family home!" My temper was flaring. I should've known better than to call her. They didn't care about anything unless it was some short-lived whim belonging to my cousins. "I don't understand why no one else cares."

"Mindy, I know you loved them, we all did, but sometimes we got to move on. Are you two still refusing to have kids?"

"It's not like it's a protest," I said. "Even if we did want kids, we couldn't afford them."

"One day you might regret it," Gail said.

"I'd rather regret not having a child than to have one and regret it."

This conversation exhausted me. At least with Gail I could say what I wanted, but why were people so determined to convince me otherwise? Complete strangers would start on the subject the moment they realized I didn't have an infant strapped to my chest. Like it was their sole duty to reach the unmaternal woman and convince her to do the right thing.

If people spent as much effort on homelessness, world hunger, or environmental change as they did my uterus, the world might be a better place.

"Well, that's the freaking truth, isn't it?" Gail said. "Far too many kids are born to shitty parents. I just think you and Christian would be good at it."

"We probably would be," I agreed. "But I'm good at downing shots of Tequila too. Doesn't mean I need to do it all the time."

After moving the conversation back to the favorite topics of what her daughters were up to, I got off the phone and went into Christian's office. When we first applied for the apartment, we asked for a one bedroom with more space, but the two bedroom (with somehow less square footage) was the only one available.

We took it because even though the second bedroom was little more than a closet, it was the perfect size for an office. It was just large enough for his desk, a printer, his computer chair and two chairs for potential clients, and a few filing cabinets. Bare, but we didn't plan on staying in the apartment long enough to do much else.

I slumped into one of the client chairs. Christian eyed me sadly. "Gail wasn't as excited as you were."

I weaved my fingers together and tried to break my hands apart to see if my tangle would hold. "She never is."

He shook his head. "It's a beautiful property. It was stupid not to buy it when they had the chance."

I groaned in resignation. Twenty years ago, that property would've cost a fraction of what it does now. But neither child would buy it even when Grandma offered it far below value to her children.

"They could've bought it and sold it later for a cool million before the market tanked, then turned around and bought it at auction again for what? Seventy thousand?"

Could have been millionaires but were determined to live anywhere else. I just didn't understand it. My aunt and uncle were not business-minded people, but unlike my mom, at least they were sane.

That night, well after Christian fell asleep, I was wide awake.

Tossing and turning in bed, the images of the farm were renewed in my mind. I thought about renovations, things I'd change. The kitchen was the perfect size, but it could use updating. New cabinets and counters, but still maintain that farmhouse feel.

My mind was full of Pinterest photos and Home Designer inspirations that were featured in Christian's catalogs.

I'd want new windows, for not only their efficiency, but also because when it got windy on that hill, the windowpanes rattled and shook so hard I used to fear that they'd break. On nights when the power went out—which was often—I'd be nestled in a pile of blankets with a flashlight waiting for the glass to break inward, slicing me to pieces.

What to do with five and half acres, though. Maybe house horses like some of the neighbors? It felt like an excess we didn't need, but I wouldn't want to give any more ground than what my grandma already had. The idea of mowing that much lawn, maneuvering around the orchard and the remains of the dairy facility. It was exhausting enough that I finally fell asleep.

When the alarm went off, I groaned. I'd just gone to sleep. A headache brimmed behind my eyes. Wonderful. I turned to confirm the empty space beside me. His side of the bed had been cold for some time. Christian was already off to work. Now it was my turn.

The biggest issue with the house had to be the upstairs. My uncle's old bedroom worked, but the bedroom my mom and aunts shared was one long stretch with a single window at the end. Practical maybe for a pack of Lost Boys, but couldn't that room be better utilized?

Might have to knock down all the walls and reformat the whole upstairs...

"... Mindy?"

I snapped my sight upward and my heart stammered. My boss stared at me like something was wrong. What?

"Yes?"

He frowned as if the response wasn't any better. Shit. I should've been paying attention. It's just hard to focus on a man with a forehead that dribbles after five minutes of conversation. "Those forecasts?"

Sitting up in my chair I focused on my computer. "They're done, I'm just waiting for the printer to be available."

Swanson made a grunt of annoyance. "You'd think we'd be able to get more than three printers."

The office had grown a lot since they took on a third partner. Being the only administrator wasn't usually an issue except for when marketing launched a new campaign. "I might just bring my printer from home," I said.

The boss scoffed at that. "No way. Just get those to me when you're able."

I smiled at him. He wasn't a bad guy as far as bosses went. I really had no qualms with my job other than it was boring work. Not nearly as exciting as helping people design their homes. But unlike my husband's business, this had a full bevy of much needed benefits.

At lunch time, I ate my turkey sandwich and checked my phone to find that Christian had texted me.

"Babe, what's with all the fire escapes around the second story?"

I smirked. Wiping the mayo off my cheek before smearing it on a napkin to text back. "A neighbor's house burned down and only the father escaped. After that, Grandpa went a little crazy with the emergency precautions."

"OIC."

I didn't mention the part where my mom often used the escape as a means of sneaking out at night to party. She and Gail always regaled in this act of rebellion and reminded one another with a single phrase like "Keg stands," or "Tyler Monroe" around Grandma, but she always knew when they snuck out. Two giggling girls were hard to miss in a mostly uninsulated home.

She never told them, so I didn't either.

"Any idea on what happened with the bathtub?" I asked.

It took him longer to respond than I liked. The bouncing dots always gave me anxiety.

"Everything is old, but there's no contamination from what I can see."

Dammit. Christian didn't want to disprove Amy and the kids' experience. That would be my bad news to relay. Might as well say "*I don't believe you.*"

He followed up with another text saying, "But the tiles are stained so bad. I could see why they thought it was blood."

"What could cause that?" I asked. Only five minutes remained of my lunch. Time to go back to work. I folded up the garbage before throwing it in the trash. I didn't check his response because I already knew the answer. He didn't know.

What looks, smells, and stains like blood? The answer was simple when it wasn't raining from the showerhead, coming from a clean well of water.

Five minutes to five, I powered down everything and eagerly waited for everyone to leave the office. I drummed my fingers at my table, eyeing the two from marketing as they carried on a conversation far longer than necessary.

One of my many responsibilities was locking up the office at the end of the day. I couldn't do that until everyone left. Sometimes my boss stayed late, he had his own set of keys, but these were the marketing goons.

"Hey guys," I said. "I need to lock up the office."

One of them checked their phone before giving me a shitty look. *Time to go... Some of us have places to be*. I wanted to meet up with Christian at the farm after work and help him any way I could. It was the least I could do since he was doing the work for free.

I closed the front door and locked it. I gave it a good yank to make sure, and then I barreled down the freeway. Inhaling with a sense of superiority, I grinned as the traffic slowed to a crawl heading south while I cruised north at full speed.

This could be my commute one day. While everyone else headed in one direction, I would be free of the daily grind. No backups or narrow mergers. The stretch ahead was dotted with speeding cars miles away. Gail said I needed to move on but moving forward was much more appealing.

5

BOOGEYMAN

C hristian's silver Toyota Tacoma was still parked in the driveway. Just the sight of it had me breathing easier. My grip on the steering wheel relaxed as I pulled up beside it. Some people are assertive enough that they wouldn't give an unprompted visit much thought, but I'm not one of those people. The pretense of helping my husband with his work was a loose slip of an excuse. I just hoped Christian informed them of my arrival.

First things first, we had to make sure that whatever happened with the bath wasn't going to happen again. I wouldn't like it if the shower rained blood on me either. If what Christian suspected was true, the family had a serious problem on their hands. I thought it was far-fetched, but he had worked with more wealthy people than I had. The kind of people who wouldn't flinch at underhanded tactics if it meant being able to sell their house for more.

Most of the clients the firm took on were people injured in car accidents. While I didn't work with them directly, I heard tales of the shit insurance companies did to try and wiggle out of compensating the injured party. So, it shouldn't have been all that surprising to learn that wealthier neighbors drive out the poor in their own ways.

Charity and Lacy came running out of the house towards me. On reflex I tensed, uncertain on how to respond. Both had silly little grins on their faces, so they must've been happy to see me. As a teenager, the brother was expectedly aloof. At his age, I used to stay in my room until haggled out. I doubted we shared the same reasons, however.

I park next to the truck and get out. "Hi, girls."

"Hi!" One of them said. I couldn't remember which name belonged to who, but I'd figure it out eventually.

"Do you two know where my husband is?"

The smaller one grinned like she was about to say something silly, swaying back and forth with her hands behind her back. There was a trace of what appeared to be chocolate around her mouth.

The older one, dressed as though she had just returned from school said, "He's in a hole."

There was a moment where my smile hesitated. I imagined the worst, but then I realized children spoke with words they know. Besides, this was Christian we're talking about. Any time I visited him on sites, he was on roofs, tall ladders, or in holes.

"Can you show me?"

The younger one took my hand, and they led me behind the goat pen where my husband was indeed in a hole. Not a deep one, just uncovering the septic trench field. "Hi, honey," he said, wiping his forehead with his gloved hand.

"What are you doing?" I asked.

He frowned at the normal appearance of the trench. "I was hoping to see some of that red stuff they were talking about. If it ran through the shower, it had to go down the drain. If not in the septic, maybe in the trenches."

I looked at the girls who stood side by side, smiling at Christian. The littlest one began to sway again. "Nothing?"

He shook his head before turning to the girls. "Can you two get your dad? Tell him it's time to cover up the trenches."

They fled with a giggle that made me laugh. "I think they have a little crush on you."

His tank top showed off his physique honed from labor. His shoulders were capped with muscle and coated in just the right amount of dirt. Glancing down at himself, he scoffed at the notion. Men have no idea what makes them attractive.

"How've things been here?" I asked, moving closer.

His eyes went to the house for a moment, Christian hesitated before saying, "I was checking out the plumbing when the youngest was down for a nap. She had a nightmare and the way she screamed... Amy said it happens all the time now."

Folding my arms over my chest, I rocked on my heels. "Maybe she's having a hard time adjusting. They moved across states, after all."

Christian nodded. "I can't find anything wrong. Just old."

His job was full of these instances. The last set of apartments, a previous tenant had been a hoarder. Each time he found another problem, the owners would curse and complain that the insurance wasn't enough to cover it.

A little girl with bad dreams and maybe a penchant for playing with food dye stirred up a lot of trouble and anxiety for the family.

Robert hailed us as he came around the shed. Wearing red plaid already. Next would be the Birkenstocks. "Everything look good?"

"Just like it should," Christian said. "I have to stop at another site—"

"I got this," Robert said, taking hold of the shovel with his bare hands and rubbing the back of his neck. "I don't know what's going on here. The whole family is walking on eggshells. Even Paul is acting weird. Just can't seem to figure out why."

"When I was the same age, I cut my bangs to here," I said, holding my index finger to my scalp.

"Did you blame the boogeyman?" Robert asked with a grin.

"I wish I was that inventive. I was still holding the scissors."

His grin faded. "Charity says it's the boogeyman. Says he's always in her dreams."

Something about that unsettled me to the point of contention. What was it about my home that had them all so uneasy? This house had held so much warmth and love for me. When I cut my hair, Grandma only laughed and used her old video recorder to tape my unconvincing testimony.

"I know I'm asking a lot, but maybe if you could take the girls around the house, tell them about your life here. Maybe it would help."

Honestly, I was hoping he'd ask. It would allow me more time in the house, and I'd get to share my favorite stories again. If the girls learned my experiences and how wonderful they were, it might be enough to banish the boogeyman.

"I'd love to."

Lacy and Charity trailed a consistent four feet behind me as I gave them a tour through my childhood. We started outside where I pointed at the greenbelt. "There's a creek at the bottom," I said. "You can catch frogs and bugs."

The littlest one stared up at me in awe. "Frogs?"

"That's right," I said. "Sometimes even tadpoles in the summer."

The older sister's nose crinkled, but she wasn't disinterested. Peering over the sloped greenbelt as though she were considering something. "You have to be careful on this road," I said. "Drivers like to speed up and down it because it's so straight."

"How old were you when you lived here?" Charity asked.

"About your age," I replied. "One time, a car hit a mother racoon, so my grandpa came out and saved her baby. So, for a time I had a pet racoon until he was old enough to send to an animal sanctuary."

"What's a sanctuary?" Lacy asked.

"It's a special place for animals to go and live in the wild without getting into trouble."

At the mention of pets, Lacy once again perked. "What other kinds of pets did you have?"

I laughed at that. "Well, on a farm you can have almost any pet you like. My mother had a pet cow, a pony named Blue, dogs, cats... My grandfather once rescued a baby deer and he bottle fed her until she got strong enough to find her family again."

This wasn't the full story, but I wanted to make it easier for the girls to understand. In truth, Grandpa did rescue a doe separated from her mother, but the neighbors didn't like the idea of a wild animal prone to ticks around dairy cows. He ultimately had to surrender her to a wildlife reserve.

"Did your Grandpa save all the animals?" Charity asked.

We walked to the goat pen and watched them for a while. They were all tuckered out and sleeping without pajamas. "Well, my grandparents loved animals and children very much."

"If you love this place so much, why did you move?" Lacy asked. As the older sister, she was clearly less afraid of asking the hard-hitting questions. The bluntness of her question set me off balance.

"If I didn't move away, you couldn't live here now."

Both girls exhibited the same dimpled cringe of uncertainty. They didn't like my answer. I supposed they wanted to be big girls and know the truth. I wanted to be careful. The last thing these two needed was to hear my grandfather died in their house.

"My grandparents were old," I said. "They couldn't take care of this big place all by themselves anymore."

This seemed to satisfy their curiosity enough. I took them to the backyard that overlooked the mountains. "They planted all these trees and the deer would come and eat the fallen apples."

"And now we have lots of trees!" Charity said, waving her hands at the rows of trees that went to the edge of the property.

"We used to have so many cows," I said. "All the cows lived where the apples are growing now."

I left out the part about how popular the fields were at night, but I smiled at the thought of all the shroom pickers. Again, all well before my time, but one old lady neighbor would wander into the fields and help herself to the hallucinogenic mushrooms that grew in the cow manure.

Leaning down to meet the girls' height, I said, "Want to see where we kept our secret treasures?"

The sisters bounced up and down and let out high pitch cries of excitement. What little girl didn't like a secret?

They lead me to their bedroom. I already knew they took up residence in the bedroom my mother and her sisters once called home. A stretch of room far too large for just two little girls. Charity still used a toddler bed placed closer to the door. All the way in the back, Lacy's twin-size bed pressed against the wall with the sole window. Narrow and cave-like, their bedroom was larger than my first apartment.

The family just moved in, granted, but it felt so empty. The girls had dressers and toys. Each had an appropriately sized vanity but the space between felt too divided. A scatter of coloring projects and a few toys. That's all.

The closet stood in the corner opposite Charity's bed. Built outward, nothing special, but I pulled the rolling doors back and pointed to the end. After all this time, it hadn't been patched up. The board with a single nail at the top.

"Now," I said. "It's very important you don't step into it. It's not meant to walk around in, but there are shelves along the sides. You can put stuff on them."

Charity shook her head. Her voice high with warning. "No," she said, pointing her small finger in accusation. "He's in there."

Pity tensed along my neck and down my spine. The color milked from her round little face. I stopped and stared, jarred by her reaction. Tensing, I stood ready to defend them, but from what?

"Who's in there?" I asked.

"The Boogeyman."

I turned to Lacy for an explanation. "She says he lives there."

"Have you seen this Boogeyman before?"

Lacy used the tip of her shoe to scratch at her lace socks. "I saw something, but I don't know if it was him."

Charity turned on her sister then. "You did see him! You saw him and then you told Mommy you didn't. Why do you always lie!"

The betrayal in her voice broke my heart. I wished I had a sister to turn on me. They had no idea how lucky they were. "Hey," I said, kneeling before Charity. "Your sister isn't trying to lie. Sometimes people get scared and don't know what to do."

"She saw him," Charity doubled down. "She saw him first."

Lacy's eyes fell to the floor while she scratched at her leg with her other foot. What was going on in her mind? Guilt or worry. A bit of both tangled up in uncertainty and fear of judgment. Poor things.

"It's just a big thing, seeing something you don't understand," I said, taking her hand. "Can you tell me what he looks like?"

Once again, Charity looked to Lacy as if waiting for permission, but it was Lacy who spoke. "He's smaller than Mommy and Daddy, but old and mean looking."

I needed to sit down. That was oddly specific to the only person who'd ever died in the house. My stomach waffled like it couldn't decide to upchuck or not.

"He smells really bad," Charity whispered.

"What does it smell like?" I asked, still clutching her hand.

"Like Great Aunt Maggie's house," Lacy said. "I can't always see him, but I can smell it sometimes. And it gets really cold sometimes."

I had a sneaking suspicion I knew what Great Aunt Maggie's house smelled like. Memories of childhood came flooding in. Keeping my clothes at Grandma's apartment or in garbage bags so the kids at school didn't tease me for reeking of old cigarettes. Apartments Christian had to treat with chemicals and special paint to treat the nicotine stains on the walls. The smell of a consummate smoker.

Rising to my feet, I told the girls to stay put while I went into the closet. The door was smaller than I remembered. Sliding the wood to the side I stuck my head in the space between the walls and took a big whiff.

Cigarette smoke. Old and stale but reeking like Mom's house. It wasn't just nicotine and secondhand smoke that could stain a house. Once people knew it was okay to smoke in a house they would light up one after another. They would drink. They'd punch holes in the walls and leave garbage on the ground. If the owner didn't care, why should they?

The stink of nicotine stained the crawlspace. The girls were getting traces of it with every draft. That whole section wasn't insulated. Wind must've pushed right through the gaps and sent the smell through the closet.

A little nicotine sealing paint and some insulation, and this ghost would be taken care of. Shaking off the description of their ghost, it was easy to reason how an old house could play tricks on a couple of little girls.

"You know what," I said, putting my hands on my hips. "I think this is a job for Christian."

6

— • —

PEDESTALS & FIRE ESCAPES

"I'm rather impressed by your Nancy Drew skills," Christin said over dinner– grilled chicken breast that I'd overcooked with a side of store bought potato salad. I never was much of a cook. If Christian perceived food as something other than sustenance to get him moving, I might've been more inspired. If I made goulash every day, he'd eat it with the same cheerful enthusiasm.

At least he waited until we got home to start in on it. He had a habit of praising and bragging about me to a debilitating point. In private it was one thing, but his public accolades would make me blush so hard I'd hide my face against his chest. Sometimes I found myself awake at night wondering if I'd ever be able to live up to the version of me that existed in his mind.

He and Grandpa both had that in common.

"It was rank," I said. "But the description the girls gave of their boogeyman..."

"Wait," he said, pausing his fork. "I thought it was just Charity's boogeyman."

"I didn't want to say it in front of the parents, but Lacy sees it too."

Christian was frowning at that. It was a disturbing thought but that didn't prove anything. "It's not uncommon for kids to change their answers based on how an adult reacts to it. She saw me asking Charity more questions, so she suddenly remembered seeing it too."

"For not having any experience with kids, you sure do know a lot about them."

A burning heat spread across my face. I didn't tell him, but I took parenting classes while getting my associates in community college. There were electives I needed to burn, and who knew, maybe one day they'd come in handy.

I shrugged and forked a bit of hardboiled egg from the potato salad.

"I don't know," he said. "This boogeyman. It's weird. I'm worried about those kids."

"Me too."

They were experiencing something bad. Whether the move was harder on them than the parents let on, or something deeper than that. Either way, those girls were terrified of something. "You don't think the parents are abusing them, do you?"

Christian winced and stared at his plate. "I don't want to think that, but we can't rule it out. Either way, Robert is coming to work with me on Tuesday."

"The Hillside Estate job?"

It was a condominium recently bought up and being converted into apartments. On the surface that didn't seem like much of a transition, but it was now owned by a major company that wanted everything uniform. Bread-and-butter jobs that paid on time were always welcome.

He nodded. "I'll be working with him a lot over the next few weeks, so if there's anything sketchy about him, we'll know soon enough."

At least we had a way of maintaining a relationship with the family that didn't border on stalkerish. Like most farmers, they needed supplementary income. Robert would be working as a hand on another farm or in the line at the labor office until next spring and Christian would have been hiring from Labor Ready either way.

"You might've ended up hiring him anyway."

"That's true, only Labor Ready doesn't get a percentage this way."

Eye on the prize, that was my husband. "What are you going to have him do?"

"Haul around supplies and set up frames. Install appliances. We'll start basic and go from there. We'll be doing a concrete pour and setting up covered parking.

I nodded.

After dinner, I washed up the plates while Christian finished up some paperwork in the office. I paused to listen to the sounds of the printer before tiptoeing into our bedroom.

Kneeling beside my jewelry dresser, I opened the doors. Long silver necklaces rattled on the hooks, and I faltered for a moment. There was no reason to be embarrassed by what I was doing, but all the same, some things are private and only for me.

Opening the bottom left drawer, I took out a flat little jewelry box and opened it. Inside was a plastic beaded star sewn to a scrap of hide. Yellow, orange, white, and red beads slightly larger than granules of sand were sewn in pattern.

I took it off one of his slippers when he died.

Pressing my face to the trinket, I inhaled. If I closed my eyes and brought myself back to that place, it smelled like home. Like Grandpa. Suede and Avon perfumes. He wore Stetson Star. A rugged, manly cologne that mingled with his leathery aftershave.

The girls inadvertently described my late grandfather and it had been simmering in the back of my mind ever since. He was a short man, even by my family's standards. A childhood illness that nearly killed him saw to that.

I strained to recall just what it was. Meningitis? Grandma said his brain swelled and it took years to recover. By the time he could go back to school, he was years older than everyone else. At sixteen, he dropped out of school to join the Army.

He was a farmer at heart but always imagined himself a cowboy.

Towards the end of his life, the hard work and childhood illness caught up to him. Stiff ankles and a slight hunch from constant back pain. He used to shuffle around the house in those suede slippers with one sunset star atop each foot.

Grandma said he never went barefoot around me because he was ashamed of the tattoos he got in the military. He had a rooster on one foot and a pig on the other. Some kind of dirty joke I wouldn't have understood anyway.

As an adult, I get the joke, but he was a farmer. Having farm animals on his feet wouldn't have been weird to me. Then again, it probably wasn't about what I understood so much as what I'd say to others.

Like the ducks with an F all over again. And I really liked pointing out ducks when they landed in the cow trough.

"Hey, honey," Christian called from the other room. "Where's the ink cartridges?"

The box snapped shut and I tucked it back into the jewelry stand and hurried off to help him. Refills were in the hallway closet, and that's where he was, but for whatever reason he couldn't see them.

I reached up and pointed. On the only shelf in the closet was a cardboard box filled with miscellaneous office supplies. Ink cartridges being one of them.

"Oh, there they are."

Even with a sign, I don't think he'd see it until I showed him. I once saw a comedy skit online where a man was calling a helpline because he didn't want to admit to his wife that he couldn't find something.

Christian laughed when I showed him, but I don't think he found it quite as funny as I did.

"I'm going to be at this for a while," he warned.

"That's fine, I'll just watch some TV."

By watching TV, I meant scrolling through my phone trying to look up the previous owners of the farm. Not an easy thing to do. The marred history of declining value and short sales, but no reason as to why people left in such a hurry.

Frowning, I noted that one person only lived there for three months and took a ten grand loss on the sale to the next owner. Then there was that person that left a brand-new tractor in the barn. Who leaves a twenty-five thousand piece of machinery behind like that? Then again, judging by the Range Rovers and the banked luxury fishing boats in the neighbor's driveways, maybe there was more money than sense. Or the loss was simply worth taking.

If the auction house failed to mention the protected silo in the middle of the property, I could see how an investor would scrap the whole property as a loss and leave. Being unable to tear down what was, honestly, an eyesore might've been a dealbreaker. They could take the barns down, level the trough, but they would still have a silo wrecking all the best laid plans. No one wanted a MOD Pizza adjacent to a collapsing silo.

So, the property remained a ghost of its former glory days thanks to endangered nesting owls.

The Miles family didn't have to worry about it since they were farmers on soil meant for farming. Still, it was uneasy to scroll through the farm's record that was quickly becoming worse than my mother's.

It was late when Christian crawled into bed. He was going to feel that come morning.

My mind was still whirling with the day's events. What the little girls' saw and the questions left unanswered. "I didn't mention that the girls claimed they saw the boogeyman around their parents," I confessed in the dark.

"Good thinking," he said. "Did he have claws and eyeballs in his hands?"

"No," I said, trying to focus on the light streaming from the light post outside. "He's a small, old man."

I could feel the air between us change. Hesitation. A twist in the current. "You think they were describing your grandpa?"

Opening my mouth to say no, I found that I couldn't. At the same time, the answer wasn't yes either. What did I think?

"I don't know. I didn't tell them anything. The last thing they'd need to hear is that he died in that house."

"How did he die?"

"He was old and sickly," I said, caressing his forearm. "He had heart problems, hearing problems, back problems. He had a massive heart attack in his sleep."

Christian knew the rest. Why I mourned my birthday that felt like a curse, and the rapid change that came after. What I didn't tell my husband, what I told no one, was the truth.

I was the death of my grandfather.

7

— · —

OBSESSION

"Mindy... Earth to Mindy..."

I jolted at my desk. Hand still on the mouse like I was doing something. What was I doing? Not sleeping. My eyes were still open while I scrolled over parcel details of the farm. Christian had finished the apartment complex and he was talking about converting the rec room into a master bedroom. There was enough room to build a bathroom and walk-in closet. He was pretty sure the plumbing ran directly under the house, but if it didn't, it would be out of budget for the family...

"Mindy?" The voice was more insistent. In the back of my mind, I understood my boss was annoyed. I wasn't working on anything company related.

"Sorry," I said. "I was just so focused."

But I wasn't, though. It was like I was tuned out or running on a different frequency. Sometimes I get this feeling at night. Like I'm asleep but it's so light that I'm aware of it. Rather than wake or fall into a deeper sleep, I just sit there buzzing like an old radio waiting for a signal.

My boss's face was a frowning, deeply troubled expression. "Is everything okay at home?" he asked. "You've been so distracted these last few weeks."

Wheeling myself away from the computer monitors, I faced the boss. "I'm really sorry. Christian's business is a full-time thing now."

"He finally left?" There was a bit of a grin then. Everyone had been waiting for him to take the leap for some time now, but Christian wanted to make sure that he had enough jobs lined up first. Recently signing for two more, we were in over our heads.

"He was so worried there'd be no work," I said. "Except now there's too much to keep up with."

The smile and glimmer of pride in his eyes faded then. As if he were reminded that this office wasn't a place for hopes and dreams of financial freedom and entrepreneurship. "We're getting some complaints. Stuff is coming in late, last week a check didn't get filed completely…"

My gut went liquid as I realized what he was saying. I was fucking up. There was only so much my job was willing to put up with.

"No, you're totally right." I agreed. "I need to focus on my job."

And not the farm.

He was nodding, but I got the impression that he didn't believe me. "I really need you to buckle down, okay?"

"I will."

"Okay."

Swanson left my area and I wanted to slink into a dark corner to hide. The cubicles around me were silent and the clicks and clacks of keyboards slowly began to resume. This was going to be watercooler gossip if it wasn't already. Yeah, Christian's business was off to a booming start, but if I got fired, we'd be without benefits.

If he got hurt on the job, or needed another root canal, we'd be in trouble.

Returning to my computer, I exited out of the seven different tabs I had open, all pertaining to the farm. What was wrong with me? I wasn't even focused on Christian's work. I was obsessed with the farm. The renovations I wanted to do and the permits I'd need to do them. This wasn't my home, but ever since I stepped foot on the property it was like I couldn't leave.

Pulling up the forecasts and accounts receivable, I had to set it aside. We depended on my stable income for a safety net. Should Christian's work slow down as most construction bids did during the wet winter months, we would need to tap into our savings.

It was a hard walk up the stairs to the apartment that evening. My legs were heavy and when I sank into the couch, it was like the pressure to succeed only mounted on my shoulders. When Christian emerged from his office to get a beer, he paused to face me.

"Bad day?"

I wanted to play it cool. To not be an additional burden, but it was like his eyes saw right through me. My throat went all tight and hot and my face did that thing where it twisted before the sobs came.

"They're going to fire me!"

It came out all dripping and sad. There I was, a grown woman crying because I couldn't get my act together. I had been working at that firm for six years. Back when it was just one attorney and a paralegal. No marketing, not even a tech guy. It was a steep learning curve going from secretary to Human Resources and Accounts Receivable. I worked there longer than my boss— only by three months, but still.

Christian sat next to me on the couch and pulled me in for a hug. "You want to watch a movie?" he asked.

"Yeah," I squawked.

He handed me the remote. "Anything you want."

What I wanted was a distraction. Something to help me set aside my fixation and worry. Something sweet, but not corny. Nothing relating to farms, little girls with nightmares, or being successful. I settled on an uplifting romantic comedy. Funny, low stakes, and not the American Dream.

And Christian was enjoying himself. He laughed when I didn't. Sipped his beer and appeared wholly content to spend this time together. It took me some time to relax, but after a third of the film, I too was drinking a beer and laughing at the jokes. My chest eased and everything was lighter.

Yes, I had been distracted at work. Shit happens. I had to forgive myself and do better, that was all.

After the film and a solid good romp in bed, I fell asleep hard. So hard that I forgot to put my phone on silent. Bolting upright, alarmed by the ringing, I scrambled on the nightstand and answered without seeing who it was.

"Hello?"

"Mindy, something happened."

"What?"

I was so disoriented. The alarm in my voice was enough that Christian was up and wide awake. He took the phone, glancing at the name on the caller id before saying, "Amy, what's wrong?"

She was crying. Not like "oh I fucked up at work and might be on my period" bad, it was a shuttering, fearful panic, like "someone died" bad.

"The doors..." her voice was rising on the verge of hysterics. "They blew off the hinges. I don't know what's happening."

Robert was muttering in the background while Lacy and Charity wailed. My heart was pounding in my chest. Throwing off the covers,

I turned on the lamp and got dressed. I wasn't waiting for Christian to get off the phone. He could stay on it while I drove over.

"Okay, we're on our way," he promised.

"I'm sorry... I didn't know who else to call."

The pale, cool snagging sensation urged my fingers on the shoelaces. Of course they called us. They didn't have family here. They were all alone in the house that occupied my every thought. Something was wrong, but I didn't understand how or why.

"Did she say anything else?" I asked as Christian got on the highway.

He shook his head. My mind went to what she said. Doors blowing off the hinges. Like, on their own? Or did Robert launch into an uncharacteristic fit? The chill of the early morning was working its way down my spine.

When Christian and I first got married, I had these dreams where he'd become a totally different person. Some women had cheating nightmares, but mine were haunted with an unreasonable, selfish, and cruel man who wore my husband's face.

I'd wake the next morning and find myself still raw from his actions in my dreams. How immovable he was to my pain as he carried on destroying our life like it meant nothing. I'd plead and beg, asking him why he didn't love me anymore, but I didn't matter.

"When we pull up, I want you to stay in the car until I get you," he instructed. The roughness in his voice caught me off guard.

Christian never *told* me what to do. There was something so comforting about it. Like he could read my thoughts and understood my fears. I hated assuming Robert was the culprit, but he was a large man and physically capable of hurting people if he wanted to.

And the truth was that men were capable of terrible things.

My dreams featuring Evil Christian reflected stories of men snapping on their wives. One-sided situations that were read in monotone voices on TikTok where men just decided to be assholes. The truth was that we didn't know Robert because we didn't know the hearts of men until they reached the breaking point.

I was Christian's priority. My safety was his biggest concern. So when he parked the car, I remained in the passenger seat with my phone open and ready to call the cops if need be.

He didn't make me wait long.

Christian was in the house for all of a few minutes before he stepped outside the front door to motion me inside. Unlocking the doors, I passed him in the entryway to find the whole family huddled on the sofa. Robert was holding both girls. Little Charity was shivering in her sleep despite being swaddled in a pale knitted blanket.

Paul was pacing the living room with a Maglite in his hand as if he wished someone would try him. Adolescent pride and protectiveness over his baby sisters while Amy stroked Lacy's long brown hair.

"What happened?" I breathed.

Robert's eyes were wet with fear. He opened his mouth to speak but Paul cut him off with an angry snarl. "I'll show you," the boy said, pointing the flashlight towards the stairs.

"Is the power out?" Christian moved to use the light switch and answered his own question.

Power outages were common on the hill. It took days for the city to come and restore it, but when I looked out the massive windows, I could see the distant lights from the neighbors. Only this property was affected, and it wasn't windy or rainy.

I'd never admit it to anyone, but Christian is afraid of the dark. I took out my phone and turned on the flashlight before handing it over to him. There was a silent acknowledgement between us. Little considerations made a marriage. For everyone else, he was shining the light on the stairs so I wouldn't trip. Buffered between two men and two sets of light.

While I knew this house better than my own soul, I knew the dark far better.

Following Paul up the stairs, he took us to the girls' bedroom. The door was on the vinyl floor. Some tacky, cheap upgrade from another owner, but it was better than the orange carpet from the seventies that my grandparents got on discount.

He aimed the beam toward the hinges. The frame was shattered around the drywall. Splinters of wood shot outward from where the hinges once were, screws and all.

I gasped. "From the inside?"

The girls were too little to have done this. Even a combined effort couldn't take down a solid wood door. There was only one person I knew who could rip a door off like this. The hinges were still attached to the door and creaked as I stepped on it.

I moved past Paul and went right to the closet. An arm looped around my waist, ready to swing me out of danger.

"There's no one here," Paul confirmed. "I've checked twice."

"Someone was here," Christian said.

"Not according to dad." The bitterness in Paul's voice was amplified in the dark. "He said it was just the wind."

"You heard it happen," I said. I meant to ask, but why ask the obvious?

"I had my headphones on," the teen's voice trembled. "I felt it. There were three bangs on the door before it fell. The girls were screaming. I—"

Paul stopped and turned away as his voice hitched. I wanted to go to him and hug him, tell him he was a good boy and an even better brother, but I didn't want to make it weird. Teenagers were standoffish. Christian stepped in and clasped a hand on his shoulder. Man to man.

Unweaving my husband's grip on the phone, I took it and aimed for the back of the closet and choked on my own breath.

The board that concealed the hiding spot was ripped off the nail and on the ground. The smell of cigarette smoke seeped through the fresh paint from the crawlspace as dark brown stains seeped through.

8

PUNCHING HEIFERS

G athered around the dining room table with a fresh pot of coffee, we sat in our own thoughts of disbelief. I wavered somewhere between denial and the inexplicable. That couldn't have happened, but it did. Was my grandfather really haunting two little girls? No. It was what Christian said. Someone was harassing the family. It had to be. I went rigid against the tides of rage that pelted me, threatening to knock me over. Kids should always be off limits.

"One hell of a wind..." Robert started, but his words faltered when everyone stared at him with varying degrees of disapproval. Amy carried the girls into their bedroom and shut the door. She either couldn't bear to hear his rationalizations or understood they were fighting words for Paul.

"The wind couldn't do that, Dad," Paul's tone suggested he was talking to anyone but his father.

It was a glaring point of contention between them. Somewhere around four am, there was an explosion of wood before Paul heard three bellowing slams against the girls' bedroom door before the door launched itself over a foot away.

At first instinct, Robert went with the most rational explanation, but in the dawning light of day, it was perhaps the least rational.

"If not the wind," Robert lowered his head. "What are we talking about? A ghost?"

"We've been trying to tell you!" Amy emerged from the bedroom. Next in line to berate the poor man. "The shower, the weird smells, the shadow the girls keep seeing. Something else is in this house."

"Or someone who wants to scare the shit out of you," Christian said.

At that, everyone looked at me for an explanation for some reason. Like I knew something they didn't. I hesitated, wondering if I was to cast the deciding vote on a haunted house or back up Christian's idea.

"Christian suspects someone is trying to screw with you," I said. "Trying to get you to leave to drive down the price on the property even further."

"Old houses like this often have massive crawlspaces. Easy to get in and cause chaos if they wanted to," Christian added.

But were they strong enough to knock down a door like that? Not likely. But he was probably right. It's not like my grandparents showed me the blueprint.

Robert lifted his head at this notion. "There was another bidder," he said. "I guess he was really angry when we outbid him. Called and complained, even."

"You didn't tell me that," Amy seethed.

Robert shrugged. "I didn't think it mattered."

With his lanky arms crossed around his chest, Paul was having none of it. "We all heard the door come down. Even a swat team would need one of those things…" he motioned like he was swinging something. "You know what I mean."

I did, but I didn't know what it was called either, but I think we all got the idea. Paul was right, but it was all so bizarre. My mind couldn't fathom a door-smashing ghost, and while I was only guessing, I was pretty sure no one else was ready to accept that either.

"It did come from the crawlspace," I said.

Amy buried her face in her hands and started to weep. "They were so scared..."

At that, we all went silent.

Another salty wave bashed through me. My own maternal instincts or the hatred for the helpless rage of seeing children crying for no reason. Whatever it was, the girls didn't deserve this.

"We can't stay here," Paul said.

"This is our house," Robert stopped short of hitting the table with his fist. At the last moment, he paused as if he realized the last thing anyone needed was another banging noise. "If someone is trying to make us leave, I'm not going to let them win."

"At the expense of our safety?" Amy railed.

"We'll move the kids to the rec room," Robert said. "Paul, I'm sorry, but I need you to share a room with your sisters."

To his credit, Paul took that in stride. I fully expected eye rolling or an argument, but he nodded in agreement. Movies always portrayed teenagers as moody, irrational twats. This kid wasn't like that at all. Christian had a swathe of younger siblings, their existence marked by the occasional calls and updates online. A few were gearing up for college. They often spoke of visiting but never did.

"That room was a later addition to the house," I said. "I don't imagine there is any secret basement or crawlspace."

"Okay, I'm just going to ask it," Amy said.

"Amy—" Robert tried to stop her, but his wife motioned to him with her hand like it was the last straw and that he'd better not try to stop her.

"Did you experience anything like this when you lived here?" Amy was looking at me.

I sat back, realizing this was why they were so eager to meet us in the first place. It wasn't because they were an all-welcoming farm family or because they wanted my tips and advice for renovations. They wanted me to confirm their fears.

Ulterior motives laid bare, I found myself reconsidering just how much I had invested in them. They only tolerated me. They needed Christian's generous offer of work. Maybe the house understood something I didn't and was trying to drive them out.

"No! Of course not." I put my hands under the table so they couldn't see them tremble. How dare she accuse me or my family. Already tense and braced for a fight and an interrogation wasn't helping. "This place holds so many good memories for me."

Amy eased at that, but Robert's face was a bright red and he couldn't make eye contact. I glanced at Christian and already knew; he was struggling to maintain composure.

As the name suggests, his parents were sometimes religious people. I say sometimes, because they didn't go to church and sort of quoted the Bible out of context when it suited them. It was more like a way to bolster their opinions when logic refused. My husband saw it for the hypocrisy that it was and became a devout atheist to spite them.

I didn't exactly subscribe to any belief or idea beyond what I could see for myself. Ghosts or evil entities were things only seen on a screen. I was fascinated by the stories based on true events. Possessed dolls and exorcisms made for creepy movies, but whenever I tried to look deeper, it was all just bunk.

But the fear in the house was genuine. That much I understood. The little girls shivering in their sleep and the teenage boy willing to share a room with his kid sisters to keep them safe— those were very real things.

"Here's what we're going to do," Christian said. "We have some work lined up in the morning, but the afternoon is open. We're going to search this house inside and out. Cover all the bases and make sure there's no sign of trespassers."

Even if Amy did think the house was haunted, I could see her shoulders relax with the idea. My heart was so conflicted. One minute I felt betrayed and the next, I wanted to reassure her that everything was okay.

"I need to go to work," I said. The twinge of yesterday's conversation with Swanson made itself known. "But I'll stop by after work and see what's going on."

"Paul," Robert asked. "Can you stay home from school?"

"Yeah, there's a test I'd like to skip anyway."

Amy shot her son a scowl as Christian's face struggled to contain the inappropriate laughter. Just when I thought he was too mature to be a high schooler...

That's when the snicker escaped my mouth. I tried to stop it, but one look at Christian bursting at the seams and it was all over. Amy held out the longest before she too was unable to ignore the much-needed humor after a harrowing night.

We went home for some breakfast. Sitting in the shower, I thought about the stories Grandma often told me about Grandpa. Her opinions of him shifted over time. After he died, she only spoke of how kind he was to animals. How he would buy the same item for each daughter and built toyboxes with extra wide gaps in case a child somehow trapped themselves inside.

As time went on and she moved away from grief, Grandma's stories took a different turn. How his disabilities made him cranky and how he railed at her. How often she considered leaving him but never did. When my great aunts encouraged her to remarry, she always said, "Once was enough."

There I sat, with my pale butter blond hair soaking in conditioner, thinking about another story she once told me.

"He punched the cow so hard; he knocked it unconscious..."

It wasn't meant to be a mean story. They had a cow that refused to go into her stall and preferred the next one. This was a major ordeal because cows liked their habits. If one got into the wrong stall, it caused a huge backup of confused heifers who wouldn't know what to do.Getting the heifer out of the stall and into the correct one was also a bit of a dance as it was a compact area, and they were big girls.

This one heifer did this seemingly out of nowhere and for months before my grandpa finally lost his patience with her. He punched the cow squarely between the eyes with enough force to knock her unconscious.

My grandfather was so embarrassed and distraught by the whole thing that he came into the house cursing, needing to take another dose of blood pressure medication because this cow nearly gave him a coronary. He told grandma what he'd done, and she went out to find the cow standing in the correct stall.

She laughed every time she told the story and I always laughed too. It wasn't until I told someone else that I realized how bad of a light it painted my grandfather. He wasn't some animal abusing monster. At least, I didn't think he was. Now I wasn't so sure.

For all the animals he rescued, there was always that poor cow that received his ire.

"He was incredibly strong. It always surprised people because he was so short," Grandma often said.

A man strong enough to render a full-grown Jersey cow unconscious with one strike could take down a door with three.

9

TIRE IRON

Christian was pacing the kitchen, dollar store coffee mug in hand. His eyes were intent like there was a discussion despite the Sunday morning quiet. He was working on something, probably something he wanted to say to me in the most tactful way possible. My stomach squirmed at the thought.

Was he going to tell me the same thing Swanson did? That I needed to get my act together and focus on the more important things. A problem with a company not paying or maybe he just woke up and decided he didn't love me anymore.

I hated how my brain jumped to conclusions.

He did a double take and smiled. "Morning. I made you some coffee."

As I sat at our garage sale dinette table sipping the coffee, I watched him forget all the important points he had intended on opening with. His jaw twitched as he reassessed the mood, calculating the best course of action. I couldn't handle it. The squirming in my stomach was rioting towards my chest.

"Spill it," I said.

He frowned as the words tumbled out. "I didn't like the way Amy came at you. It's not your fault they're going through... Whatever."

All the worry evaporated, and I was able to sip my coffee loaded with creamer. He was being protective. Scratching at a rough patch on the top of my wrist, I thought about how to explain how it made me feel.

Like a tire iron in the back of the trunk under the spare. A specific tool that has no other use. No matter how important and wanted a tire iron is in the moment of a flat tire on the side of the freeway. The rest of the time it's eyed as something taking up much needed trunk space.

It's not the first time I've experienced this sort of transactional relationship. I think most people have. When I needed someone to resemble a mother figure, I called Gail. I liked our postman right up until my package landed on my neighbor's door. This is apartment thirty-two, Jerry, I thought we had a rapport by now.

Still, admitting the true extent of my feelings could backfire. Christian wasn't someone who took half measures. Especially not when it came to me. If I let him know just how used I felt — almost blamed — by the Miles family, his retribution would be swift.

He'd tell Robert there were no more jobs that required his help. Returning to the farm would be difficult if not impossible after that. It might be for the best. Ever since we were invited in, it was like I couldn't leave. I was more surprised Christian wasn't going to talk about my infatuation with nostalgia than anything.

"She was upset," I said, treading carefully. "It didn't feel great. It was almost like she was accusing me of withholding information."

"You're not under any legal obligation to disclose anything," Christian reminded.

"I know, and I wouldn't mind telling Robert and Amy that my grandfather died in the house, I just didn't want to say it in front of the little girls."

The left side of his lip turned in a slight grimace. "I can only guess that they would appreciate that, but that's my point. You are so sweet and kind. Considering their feelings when it didn't feel like Amy was considering yours at all."

I nodded. Not wanting to dismiss his spot-on assessment. "It felt like that, but someone was in their daughters' room, punching down their door. So, I don't really blame her."

Christian winced. What was going on in his mind? His eyes were fixed on the cup of black coffee in his hand before saying, "This isn't our problem."

It hit me like the metal frame of a tennis racket to the back of the skull. Between the sheer truth and the underlying context, I sat dumbfounded. He was right. This wasn't our problem. We just wanted to see my childhood home and meet the new owners. They wanted to know if I thought the house was haunted.

I couldn't answer that question anymore than they could. Did I even think ghosts were real? Not a clue. We were at an ideal point to create distance from a weirdly evolving and possibly dangerous situation. I worried about the girls, but it wasn't like I could protect them. They had their big brother and parents.

Worst case scenario, the family would foreclose on the farm and move. And if Christian was right (and he usually was) the person causing all this trouble would get what they're after and the family would figure it out soon enough. Maybe they could sue the person. It would be hard without proof.

I gnawed on the rounded callous along my fingernail. It was tucked in a corner just out of reach, but I clipped at the edges anyway. "I think we should at least see if we can document any signs of an intruder."

Christian was nodding before I finished the sentence. "I think that's fair."

We already had those plans with Robert. Backing out wouldn't sit well with either of us. Guilt was always something that negged the both of us. It was a common thread that stitched our hearts into one. A bleeding, thumping mass of muscle that puckered at the seams.

His heart centered around the family that resided back east in Pennsylvania. A large, involved family that couldn't understand why he refused to come home.

My guilt was a result of... I didn't quite know. The need to prove that I was worth stealing Christian away from an adoring family? No, I've always been this way. Eager to insert myself and demonstrate my generosity and kindness because it always felt like someone was watching.

Not like in the religious sense. There was no God following me around with a scale and weights. Nothing like that. It was more like other versions of myself observed and debated how they'd handle things differently.

Past me would never allow herself to get a stern talking to at work.

Jeopardizing the security of our family and the future. And for what? Some overgrown fantasy. I didn't even like the farmhouse. The layout was weird and there was only one bathroom. One root canal away from being sent to collections. Past me would've hated myself for the lapse in coverage knowing that if Christian fell off a roof or hurt himself on the job, we'd be shit out of luck.

Future me would have urged me to quit. Fuck Swanson and his constant sweating forehead. Setting up health insurance was just something Christian's company would need anyway. Like it or not, he also needed an admin. He was spending far too much time in his office at night. Wouldn't it be nice if he could just come home from work and be done with the day?

I could do that for him. He'd never ask me to because it's his company and his risk. If his company flopped it would be his failure and not mine. He'd be the one slinking back to his old job, not me. Once again, guilt was wrapping itself around everything we did.

And for what?

It was close to eleven at night when his side of the bed sank to that familiar, rightful level and allowed my whole body to ease. Finally able to breathe again and to think clearly without the nagging trepidation of the past.

"You're too busy," I said, preparing myself for what I was going to say next.

"I know. I knew it was going to be hard for us, but I didn't think I'd miss you so much."

His hand snaked around my own and my heart tremored. Here I was, so wrapped up in my own worries, it never occurred to me that Christian was fighting his own.

"That's not where I was going with this. I knew you weren't going to have time for us for a while, and I'm okay with that. What I'm not okay with, is letting you take all the risk."

Christian shifted to his side to face me. "What are you saying?"

I turned to face him. It was dark, so I had to guess where his face was, but gestures matter, right?

"I'm going to quit my job and work with you."

"What if I stop getting jobs?"

A smile was forming along my lips. "You're booked out till spring. I can hear you turning down projects because you have no one to manage them. It's not the lack of work that's holding you back. If your company fails, it's because I'm not all in."

He was quiet for a moment. Considering and calculating everything all at once. "We'd spend more time together and I'd have a project manager."

"And receptionist, marketing, paper pusher, and HR," I added. "That way, you can just do the building."

Christian was smiling. I couldn't see it, but I felt it in my bones. The way the worry and guilt evaporated from the single bedroom apartment. Yes, this was the right way to go. Maybe my fixation with the farm wasn't about the farm at all. It was me, trying to become emotionally invested in something knowing that Christian was out there doing this on his own.

The next day, I cornered Swanson in the break room. He was sipping coffee with enough aspartame to give his children's children birth defects.

"So, I thought a lot about what you said on Friday," I started, but the calm, almost relieved expression on his face made me hesitate. "I think you're right. I am too preoccupied with Christian's business."

"Imagine running your own business," Swanson said with a longing sigh. "I'd be worried if you weren't excited for him."

"Well, it's just that he needs a partner, and it's not fair to this company or him if I keep trying to do both."

"Agreed," the boss said with a nod. "This your two weeks?"

Swallowing the hard lump in my throat, I nodded.

This was harder than I expected. Future me promised it would be freeing. Defiant. Instead, I was sad and a little wistful about the whole thing. This was a company I had grown with over the last six years. Sure, the pay wasn't great, but it was stable. Car accidents always happened. Lawsuits and negotiating with insurance companies were more prevalent in recessions.

Swanson nodded and made his way back to his office before pausing. "Oh, um, hire someone on the lower end of the scale. Young and eager."

I stood alone in the break room stunned.

Was that it? I coordinated the farewell parties and exit interviews. Ordering and picking up cupcakes and rallying the troops from out of their cubicles to congratulate a coworker for moving up in the world. I made the error in assuming someone other than myself felt that it mattered.

If I was worth a damn, they might have at least offered a raise for me to stay. This company didn't give a shit. Swanson didn't give a shit, just so long as I hired someone else at a cheaper wage. Because only someone new and inexperienced would be desperate enough to cling to this job.

I must have been a sight. Nostrils flaring, muttering under my tight breath as I packed my things into a cardboard box. And to think I offered to bring my printer to work! No one noticed as my packing got louder. Don't mind her, just another cubicle breakdown. Would they even lock up or just assume I'd always be there to do it?

Shaking out the weakness trembling in my arms, I steeled my legs. It wasn't my problem anymore.

The keys sat firmly on the desk as I took my little cardboard box that contained all of six years and what it was worth, and I walked out the door.

10

— · —

WHAT REMAINS

The family had cleaned much of the debris from the incident, but there were still fragments of splintered plywood embedded in the carpeted rooms. No bare footing around here anytime soon. Whatever had caused the implosion managed to blow the door outward, leaving no trace within the secret cubby.

Let's be honest, it wasn't a secret. My grandparents built the house so they knew the crawlspace was there. They nailed the wood plank over the hole and painted it along with the rest of the room. Probably for accessibility. So my grandparents knew the space was there, and so did my aunt and mom. The only secretive aspect about the crawlspace was how it was used.

Maintenance workers probably trespassed through the area a dozen times while my aunt and mom were at school. They probably noticed the love letters from boys and other little sacred items along the beams. There would be a wry smile and a hint at what was in there, but Grandma wouldn't have disturbed their cache. She understood a girl's need for privacy.

Secrets don't know they're secrets. Like any other truth, secrets remain unchanged. They sit on dusty shelves and omitted by those who don't need them and cherished by those who do.

While truths don't typically implode in closets, they can leave human-sized spaces that leave us to wonder, "What now?"

I was in such a space, easing a scope on a long cord into the tiny crevices between boards and plywood. The tablet propped beside me revealed nothing but dust and darkness. All the things I expected.

"Any good news articles?" Christian asked, ducking into the crawlspace.

I gave him a bemused smile from over my shoulder. "What?"

"Old houses didn't exactly have proper building requirements. Sometimes people used newspaper as insulation."

"Oh, well, nothing like that in here. They must have relied on the spiders to insulate with cobwebs."

We both knew what to look for: signs of forced entry. So far, there was no sign of anything.

"Well, that's that," Christian said.

My heart ached as I pulled the snake-like cord up. There went our theory that an intruder had done it. What were we going to tell the Mileses? All three children were still sharing the rec room. Paul had partitioned a section of the room with mismatched curtains hanging from the ceiling. He took the section closest to the door and slept with an aluminum baseball bat by his bed.

Despite their elder brother's precautions, the nightmares hadn't abated for his sisters.

"Charity has been sleepwalking," I told Christian.

Amy told me in confidence earlier that morning. Lacy's crying woke Paul and the youngest wasn't in bed. "They found her in her pajamas, sitting by the oak tree."

"The rain didn't wake her?"

I shook my head. "They buried all the pets around that tree. My uncle's border collie, my mother's old tomcat."

Christian took all this information in, but his eyes flickered with recognition. "And the septic is back behind that tree."

Something like threads pulled within me then. I couldn't explain it, but it felt right. Like we were following an intentional trail, but to where? Charity was the same age as me when I lived here. Young enough to not grasp the nuances of the world around her, but sensitive enough to receive all information. Even the bits that she didn't understand.

Lost in my thoughts, I was pulling the cord faster. The camera and the light were spinning around in the first-floor ceiling. Christian squatted to retrieve the tablet when the camera rotated and illuminated something...

Christian jolted upright. He staggered and stepped on the plywood and not the beam. My breath caught and I dropped the cord to grab him, but I was too late. He fell backward. Old wood fragmented and crackled. Dust erupted and created a storm around us.

Covering my mouth with my shirt, I didn't inhale the debris, but my eyes felt like sandpaper when I blinked, and it stung badly. Fifty years of sloughed skin and anything else had coated my eyeballs like sugar on a donut. But where did he go?

"Christian?"

He didn't so much as cry out. There was a cough of surprise followed by nothing. The dust waned enough for me to open my eyes even if it felt like they were on fire. I blinked and blinked again. Christian was gone, but where?

Confusion nestled tightly within my constricted chest and aggravated airway. Had he caught himself and stepped out of the room? No. He wouldn't have left me like that.

The floor beneath the beams wasn't broken or even cracked. I didn't hear him break the dry, old wood.

Panic boiled over as I went from yelping his name to a shaky scream. Where did he go? I didn't understand. One moment he was there, and the next he was gone.

A grunt came from somewhere below me. With shaky fingers I pressed on the floorboards as if they would part the way and give him back to me. "Christian?"

My screams must've been heard across the property. Robert was calling my name and I could hear his heavy footsteps as he ran up the stairs. The farmer materialized in the makeshift doorway and stared at me. "Christian's gone?"

"I'm here." The voice of my husband was muffled, but it was there.

Mom told me that if I stepped anywhere but the beams, my weight wouldn't be supported on the weak cross sections. I'd fall through the ceiling and land in Grandpa's chair. Not the worst place to fall, though poor Grandpa would've been frantic if a small child randomly fell through the ceiling. He was so cautious, I'm surprised he didn't barricade that crawlspace in the same way they left baby locks on everything until the day we moved.

It turned out that this was not the case.

Christian's fists were banging on the floor, bumping the debris along. "It's a trap door," he said. "Push on this area."

Robert and I shared a silent exchange within moments.

What is this?

I have no idea...

Eager to get Christian out, I pressed down on the spot and the wood panels moved as one. A hand emerged from the underside to pull it down the rest of the way. It was only when his dirt-streaked face peered up at me that I could breathe. There he was. There was my home.

"I'm guessing your grandparents didn't build this," he said.

I wanted to slap him, or maybe just hug him. I wasn't sure. All I knew was that he was okay. Cracking jokes despite falling through a trap door in a crawlspace and seeing something we didn't expect.

"Did...was that a skull?" I asked.

The smile on his face waned and Robert extended his hands to pull Christian up. "We need to call the police."

Nothing quite like finding a body in a house. Well, not an entire body. Just a skull and not an accident.

The police cars came silently up the hill and parked in the driveway. They came with questions and yellow caution tape. Forensics confirmed that there was indeed human remains of undetermined age left in a space made especially for well...this.

"Any idea where the rest of the body is?" Yet another detective asked.

"No." I'd given up on trying to give embellished answers. It was going on midnight. Every so often Amy would pull Robert into their bedroom. An argument would break out before he was forced to come out and answer questions.

She wanted to leave. I did too.

"So, you were the previous owner and sold the house. Why are you here?"

The way the detective framed the question caught me off guard. Like it was me who hid a body here. "No. My grandparents built the house and sold it when I was seven."

"Why did you come back?"

My eyes ached from fatigue and probably rotted wood fragments embedded in them. I rubbed my temples and tried my best to answer the question. "We own a construction company. We were investigating their complaints."

"The septic and door issues."

I nodded. The detective lit up a cigarette and offered it, but I declined. Smoke was already filling the porch patio and I didn't want to smoke this close to the door in case someone opened it. You'd think he'd be a bit more considerate to the owners, but cops were cops.

"Did you find anything out of the ordinary?"

I blinked and the concrete patio beneath my feet made a lazy spin. How many times were they going to ask? "Septic was totally fine. We thought maybe someone was pulling a prank on the family."

"So, you were up there looking for proof when the incident happened," the detective's voice warped like a worn-out record. The tone drooped and stretched like taffy pulled across hooks. Part of my mind was screaming that something was wrong, but I had to answer, didn't I? It would look suspicious if I stopped talking, and I couldn't be suspected. Not of anything.

"But that doesn't answer my question. Why are you here, Mindy Mounts?"

The use of my maiden name jarred me back into reality. How did he know that? The space between my ribs began to tremble. Jerking my head up to look at the detective, there was only a black figure before me. Backlit by the low wattage porch light. Every bit of exposed skin stung like I was drenched in ice water.

Arms wrapped around me from behind. I let out a shriek before arching and flailing, but the grasp pulled me in tighter. "Hey," a familiar voice soothed.

I looked up to find it was Christian. Jerking back to the figure before me, the detective—or whatever it was—was gone.

"He was just there," I stuttered.

"Who?"

"The detective..." As the words came out of my mouth, it felt like a lie. He wasn't a detective, he wasn't anyone. Yet he knew my maiden name and wanted a secret from me.

"It's been a weird day," Christian said, rubbing my arms and shoulders. "Let's go home and get some sleep."

We said nothing on the drive home.

The day's events simmered on my tongue as I debated what to say and how. I never kept anything from Christian. Not the time I got drunk on too many mimosas at brunch and bought a pair of Dior sunglasses or the time I bought that special soap that only resulted in an intense rash that lasted for weeks and left scars along the back of my thighs. Not that I could lie about the soap, he was bound to see the rash at some point.

He never judged me because I was harder on myself than he ever could be. And when I couldn't return the sunglasses because they were clearance items, we ate top ramen for weeks together afterward.

This was different.

I saw something that night that either wasn't real or natural. It wasn't a matter of wanting to hide it because I thought I was going insane; it was because I didn't want him to worry. By telling Christian what I saw, I was forcing him into making an impossible choice. Believe me and the unbelievable, or wedge something that felt a lot like space between us. There's no winning in such a predicament. I'd rather us carry on together as we always had and put the incident behind me. Chalk it up to stress and fatigue.

Between leaving my job of six years, starting a new company, a shitload of paperwork, finding a human skull in my grandparent's house, Christian nearly being injured... It had been a week.

"I'm going to say this as nicely as I can," Christian said, not taking his eyes off the road. "But when we get home, you really need to take a shower. Toss those clothes directly in the wash."

Grabbing my coat, I pressed it to my nose, inhaled stale, half smoked cigarette smoke, and gagged. Rotted, wet and base, I smelled absolutely putrid. "I didn't even smoke," I said with more than a little indignation.

I rifled through my pockets, searching for the source, and found a soft rectangle in my pocket. Pulling it out, I held in my palm a soft pack of Winstons. The lip was ripped off revealing a whole pack of half-smoked cigarettes.

"An entire pack of half-smoked cigarettes? Who does that?"

Christian looked at me then. He was frowning. Yes, I lit up one every now and again, but I would never put a half-smoked cigarette back into a case. The odor alone caused me to gag. It resulted in many rants about smoking etiquette.

Never leave butts laying around, smoke near doorways or on people's property without permission, if children were around then forget it. I had a whole slew of rules, and this was number one. I smoked when I went out with my smoking friends and if I was drowning in nerves, but that was it.

Christian did a double take at the cigarettes before saying in a most apologetic tone, "I don't know anyone else who smokes Winstons."

Neither did I.

They were the only brand I smoked. Additive free, but not packed so densely as American Spirits. What was even stranger was the package. The lettering wasn't as bold but had the same red and white scheme across the front. Maybe because it was a soft pack?

"They don't even make soft packs anymore."

Christian was frowning as he mulled that over in his mind. I didn't know what to make of it either. Abstract things like injustice, poverty, abuse,those things bothered me. As far as pet peeves went, I had few. Namely one. Why the hell would someone smoke half of each cigarette knowing it smells like a can of moldy butts and put all twenty half smoked cigarettes into a pack?

It was like someone was playing a practical joke on me. Intentionally trying to grate my nerves during what was already an incredibly stressful day. Taking the jacket off, I rolled it up and tucked it between my ankles. Hopefully taking some of the odor with it.

"There were a lot of jackets hanging up," I said. "Maybe someone stuck their pack in my jacket by mistake."

It was beyond paranoid to assume someone was intentionally trying to make me smell like a soggy ashtray. No one wanted to bag up a skull and take it from a secret hiding spot in a house. Everyone, detectives included, was probably stressed and just wasn't paying attention.

He didn't say anything else until we got into our parking spot. Throwing the car in park, Christian turned to face me with a stare so intense I thought he was going to kiss me for the first time all over again.

"This is getting too weird. I don't like the idea of you going back to that house."

Christian would never tell me what to do — there were too many broken casserole dishes and patched up walls in his parent's home — so he asked. I loved him for that. He so rarely made requests, I hated to deny him.

"I feel the same way."

"Okay." It was like he needed to say it because he needed to confirm that he had asked, and I responded positively.

We had done what we said we'd do. It was more than most would've done. I wasn't willing to have Christian fall into another bizarre pit full of human remains. And as much as I liked Robert, I was in full agreement with Amy. They needed to leave. Whatever transpired after my family moved out had tainted the house. Someone was murdered in that house. It was time to pack up and leave.

I had to trust that Amy would do what was right by her family, and that Robert would come around eventually. Sure, they would take a loss on the property, but it was better than cowering in the rec room with an aluminum baseball bat and stumbling over bones.

11

MOLLY

When I was nine, the family dog wandered off, as dying animals often do.

She was a retriever lab mix in the twilight years of her life. Curved, overgrown nails that hurt to walk on, she was nearly bald from a skin infection. As much as Mom loved animals, she didn't have the energy or the resources to properly care for them. That poor miserable dog.

I liked to think she left us to find help. Maybe she encountered some good Samaritan who took her to a vet and made all her scaly patches better. A new, luxurious coat grew in, and she found a family who could afford to manage her skin condition. It wasn't that we didn't love her, she received as much care as we could afford. But it wasn't enough. We weren't enough.

But in all likelihood, Mollie wandered off to die under a patch of untended blackberries and wait for death to take her.

The kindest thing we could do after she left was to simply not get another dog. A vow broken not long after Molly's passing. As if keeping my own promise to her, I never got another dog again.

The memories invited themselves while I crossed the street towards the office supply. Someone was giving puppies away from the back of their truck. Beautiful, bouncy puppies with copper hair and wagging tails. I smiled at them. A little boy was crying happy tears with one in his arms. Would those people be able to care for the puppy when it grew old, and his skin became infected? Would they wash away the scales and lotion the dog in special ointments?

I would.

But did I have time for a dog? Working from home meant I could devote time to a dog, but there were the apartment fees and the vet bills. Those puppies would need shots and neutering.

There were three puppies left. They yelped and poked their little wet noses from the box. I went inside to buy more printer paper and tape. A few things here and there to tide us over. When Christian started the company, the first thing he bought was an accounting program. Staring at the boxes, I cringed at the prices. That was why he was so fretful in the beginning. He must've felt as though he were hemorrhaging money. I was uneasy just looking at it all, but I was eyeing the project management tool and trying to remember the balance on the company credit card.

Learning a whole new system on top of project management was a daunting prospect. Maybe next time. For now, I'd just use templates I found online.

When I emerged from the store my eyes went to the now vacant parking spot, and I exhaled. Temptation was behind me.

But I'd bring up the topic of getting a dog with Christian. Cats were less responsibility, but did he even like cats? It was bewildering to me that I genuinely didn't know. He never pressed the issue. How did I not know something so basic about him? I doubted he disliked either animal, so that's probably why I never thought about it.

Just after six I heard the front door open. I scanned the desk overflowing with paperwork. It didn't matter when I stopped. I'd make no substantial headway by working the rest of the evening. It would take weeks to get it all sorted. I knew that going into this, but there was still a pang of guilt when I left the office.

Christian was making sandwiches. One for tomorrow's lunch and two for our dinner. He turned to smile at me. "Do you want to share a soup with me?"

"No, that's all you."

We ate in near silence. He was scarfing down the sandwich like he hadn't eaten all day. When his plate was empty, I nudged mine towards him. "I had a snack earlier."

He was not one to waste a sandwich.

"How was work?" I asked.

"Good," he said, covering his mouth as he spoke. "Robert didn't want to go home, poor guy."

I couldn't blame him. "Amy is pushing to leave, isn't she?"

"He would if they could," Christian said. "But they can't afford to move. I don't think they anticipated taxes being so high."

Ugh. The taxes. I hadn't even considered that.

Even though they bought the place at auction, the taxes would be based on property value not purchase price. And while the property struggled to stay occupied, the value of the land was still higher than most.

Like it or not, the Miles family was trapped.

"I just want to know what happened. Who..."

My words trailed off, but he knew my thoughts. Creating such an odd trap door to hide a skull. Who's skull and when? We agreed to step back from the farm. There was no sign of intruders, and the police were carrying out a full investigation. There was nothing else for us there apart from my yearning.

"That farm went through a lot of hands over the years," Christian said. "Could've been any of them."

I just hoped it wasn't murder. I couldn't imagine it being anything else, but to have my childhood home tainted by something so awful put a damper on my own dreams too. Would I even want to buy the house back knowing what I did now?

The property was still beautiful, and it still had so much potential, but I'd want a new house built. Yet another pipe dream.

"So, you have several jobs lined up in Graham," I said. "I know some of them are recently contracted, but I think if we prioritized by location, things would be more efficient."

Christian was nodding as he casually checked his face for crumbs. "That will work. I need to finish the one in Sumner first. It's running late."

After dinner, we watched some TV. It was an episode where someone gave away a dog only to have the owner come looking for the pet. That reminded me...

"Would you say you're more of a cat person or a dog person?"

My husband's face went stern as he debated this question internally like I'd asked him to choose a favorite between children we didn't have. Being childless was an easy choice for us from the start, and perhaps pets were lumped into that category years ago, but now I wasn't so certain.

"Ca—no–." His eyebrows were arching along his high forehead. "Dogs? No. Cats—I don't know."

"Okay," I said, choking back my laughter. "Don't hurt yourself. I was just curious."

"Where's this come from?"

I told him about the puppies outside the office supply and the smallest of grins crept across his face. "You'd be the one taking care of it."

Insecurity tugged and Molly's deep brown eyes blinked back tears. I had enough responsibilities as it was. The whole reason I didn't want kids was the raging uncertainty that surrounded it. So many things could go wrong. Everything would change. Maybe for the better, but the future was already so vague, throwing another person into the mix didn't seem fair.

Cats didn't care about much apart from food and a clean litter box.

It was something to contemplate. To take my mind off the disturbing recent events. As I laid down to sleep that night, I tried my best to focus on kittens or puppies, but in my mind, I was standing at the base of the hill, staring up at the house.

The lights were out, and the yellow hue deepened in the dusk. I always hated yellow, but it was Grandpa's favorite color. They always painted the house a shade of yellow. Close enough to white for Grandma to tolerate, but just enough yellow to keep Grandpa from complaining.

I was dreaming.

In the place of the orchard was a hillside of green grass. A row of trees started along the backyard like when I was a kid. The peacocks tucked in their tails and nestled together for warmth as the night approached. For being such beautiful birds, they sure did make an awful noise. Somewhere between a screech and a caw, they summoned the rest of their flock.

What was I doing, standing at the crossroad?

Closing my eyes, I wished I was somewhere else as dread set in my bones. It was a dream. I just needed it to run its course. Think of puppies and kittens. A big fluffy orange tabby or a happy golden retriever...

Opening my eyes, a soft cry slipped from my lips as my old dog, Molly stood in the middle of the road.

Still patchy and nearly hairless apart from the white around her muzzle, she looked at me before heading up the road. Her long nails clicked against the pavement. It must've hurt, walking on nails that curled into the paw pads. Why couldn't Mom at least trim them? Was that so hard?

"Molly," I called, moving towards her. "Come here, girl. You can't be in the road. If a car comes, they might hit you."

She didn't hear me or was just ignoring me as she often did. So, I quickened my pace to catch up. As if it were a game, Molly's speed also increased. She was fast for an old dog. My breath was creating puffs of steam as I went after her. The only light was the single streetlamp at the crossroads, and it was getting darker with every step.

"Molly!" I said more sternly than before. I hated yelling at her knowing she deserved better. Her skin was crusted over so painfully that it was emitting pus. I should have done more. Begged someone to take her to the humane society while she still had a chance. Anything but wait for Mom to do the right thing.

"I'm sorry." My voice broke. "Come here, good girl."

Just when I caught up to her, Molly veered right. Her patch-work tail was the only clue as she disappeared behind the tall grass. I promised him I wouldn't go back. The Miles family were good people and she'd be safe from cars. There was no reason to follow Molly anymore.

But she was my dog, wasn't she? My responsibility. Leaving her for them to deal with wasn't right. She was a good dog and underneath her craggy exterior were good bones and perhaps several more years if cherished.

Acidic and jolting, a child's scream pierced through the darkness like an unexpected train whistle. An image of Charity came to mind.

Her little braided pigtails and hollow, tired eyes. Seeing Molly in the dark would've been terrifying to a young girl.

Footfalls crunching in the gravel, I ran to the old oak tree beside the goat pen. No, it wasn't a goat pen—it was a horse stall with a single pony. His fur was mangy in a way that reminded me of Molly's fur. Even in the dark I could see the ribs poking through his thin skin. Why was Blue so sickly? He was my uncle's horse, and he'd never allow the animal to be neglected. Not like Mom did with Molly.

I don't know how I knew, but there was only one place Charity could be. The place she laid her body when even sleep caused unrest. The porch light was on, and it served as the only source of light apart from the crescent moon. Stars were brighter on the hill but even here, light pollution waded the sky.

Charity was curled up all by herself. Her tiny body made cozy nooks among the exposed tree roots. Kneeling, I swept my hand over her head. Her eyes were wide open and vacant. "Molly is a nice dog. You don't need to be afraid. She's just sick."

The peacocks started cawing and flapping like an intruder had disturbed their sleep. Their cries became more frantic before the loudest was suddenly clipped short mid-scream. Alarmed and fighting... Whatever their panic, I didn't want the culprit near Charity.

"Let's get you inside," I said, scooping her up in my arms, she remained limp like a life-sized doll. I traversed the gravel driveway towards the porch light at the pace one might march through a swamp.

The weight of her body stressed my legs, and no matter how hard I tried, they refused to carry us. Sagging to the ground, I pushed myself up again and again but the house just a few yards away remained in the distance.

"Charity, get in the house."

The peacocks' screams were desperate and wild. Chased from the back of the house, birds were attempting to flee their attacker. Feathers erupted from the side door of the house as some unseen entity grabbed a male by the neck and yanked him back into the shadows.

Wincing at the snap of delicate bones and dying cries, I held Charity closer. It was too late. Whatever came for the birds was coming for us.

"Charity, please, you need to run."

I shook her but the girl remained limp, her face impassive and her eyes wide with some unknowing horror. "He already has me."

"Who has you?"

"He has you too."

"Who?" I demanded with another shake.

"The boogeyman." Her voice was slow and drawling. Like Charity's mind was already a distant thing. Abstract and lost in whatever nightmare the house had in store for her. I did the useless thing and started to cry. I couldn't help Charity any more than I could help Molly. The only thing left to do was to brace myself.

"If you want her, you'll need to get through me."

Shadows rippled through the open door, swimming toward us as it swallowed the light. I peeked for just a moment to see a familiar pair of eyes staring back at me.

12

COMPENSATION

"Babe," Christian's voice broke through the incapacitating fear that wrapped around my legs, forcing me to the ground. "Hey, wake up."

Kicking away the countless needle pricks in my legs, the sweaty sheets came away as I cursed and winced from the numbness. I'd twisted my legs so wrongly in my sleep, taking the sheet with me. No wonder I couldn't walk in my dream, my legs were asleep.

"Are you okay?"

Christian was rubbing my shoulder and stroking my neck before wiping away the very real tears. His voice was raw with concern. I tried my best to explain, but it came out all wrong.

"Molly went to the farm and Charity couldn't move. Blue was mangy and something was making the peacocks scream!"

Like air leaving a balloon, the nightmare and all the details that frightened me had deflated. What remained were erratic details and a notion that I was scared, even if I wasn't now. Just embarrassed and sweaty, rambling about a fading dream.

"Nightmare?"

Flexing my toes, the stinging subsided even if the gravelly feeling beneath the skin remained. "I was trying to think of puppies instead of the farm, but instead I dreamed of my last dog *on* the farm."

"Well, at least you tried…"

Rolling over on my side, I faced him. "I know we agreed to back off, but I'm worried about those little girls."

"I know you are, but there's nothing we can do."

Christian was right, but this worry in my heart kept suggesting otherwise. Guilt wound tight around my ribs and refused to ease. This wasn't my fight. It wasn't about me and inserting myself only made things worse. I was a plumber trying to navigate knob and tube electricity. I was a heart in the right place, but no knowledge or tools. A wrench threatening to fall into the engine.

And if I caused harm, there would be no compensation for the family.

The next morning was a groggy one, but the easy commute from the kitchen to the office was one I'd never take for granted. Still wearing Christian's slippers and a bathrobe, I got to work. Organizing all the jobs by dates due and locations, I was able to find more time on his schedule and when he texted about another potential job, I was able to add it in and email the contract over.

He'd taken care of licensing and liability insurance, but there was still the matter of our health insurance. That led to several hours of eye-drying boredom. Maybe there were some things I'd still leave up to him as the company owner.

My phone lit up with a number I didn't recognize. Normally, I'm of the mindset that if it's important they'll leave a voicemail, but what if Christian forwarded my number to a potential client?

"Hello?"

"Mrs. Lawson, this is Detective Rodrigo."

Oh, well, there was always that. Why I found it unexpected, I still don't know. We only found human remains, of course the detective would call. They said they would.

"Hi, how can I help, Detective?"

"We're following up on the remains found last week. I understand you lived there as a child."

It's never a good feeling talking to police. Even when I was obviously wasn't involved or under investigation, there's always a culpability somehow. My brain raced through all the responses given that night and whether they indicated illegal activity. The pads of my fingertips went cold, and my throat narrowed like a sieve.

"Yes?"

"Well, forensics came back and dated the remains to the eighties. Your grandparents still lived in the house at the time."

"I don't understand..." It was a good thing I was sitting, because the room dissolved like wet salt.

"What can you tell me about them?"

"They were in the process of retiring from dairy farming. Selling cows and leasing land."

"But they still lived in the house during that time."

"My grandfather died in ninety-three. Grandma sold the main property and moved."

"Mrs. Lawson, did anyone else live there in the eighties?"

I was a reservoir of memories not my own, yet even I couldn't say for certain. "I lived there from eighty-seven to ninety-three. It was just the three of us then."

"And before that?"

I wasn't born yet, so how would I know? Not the time to be catty even if it did feel like an intrusion into what I held most sacred. "I couldn't say."

"No aunts or uncles, anything like that?"

"My aunt Gail moved out of state for college in the eighties. My mom wasn't exactly in the picture at that time. My uncle moved to Vermont, but I don't know exactly when. I've never even met him."

At this, his voice softened. "Your grandparents had sole custody of you?"

"Not in the legal sense," I explained. "My mom is a drug addict. My grandparents raised me when she couldn't."

"I see. Is there any way you can talk to your aunt to explain the situation? I really need to talk to someone who lived in the house during that time."

Blowing a breath hard enough to send my bangs flying, I considered the lovely prospect of talking to Gail about the farm. She was always touchy about it before. I'm sure she's going to love that I stepped in it before trekking around her house.

"I'll call her and let her know."

Maybe researching health insurance wasn't the worst thing on my list of things to do today. Better yet, I needed to step out of the office. Get something to eat, maybe do some laundry, anything to distance myself emotionally from that phone call.

I stripped the bed sheets and even removed the duvet cover knowing how much I'd regret it later. Why was it so hard to put it back on? It was worse than trying to fold a fitted sheet. No matter how many videos I watched I was pretty sure the feat required an engineering degree.

The comforter hung over the porch railing while I collected every towel, clean or otherwise and soaked them in bleach water in the bathtub.

The whole apartment hummed from the washer and dryer as I took baskets of ignored clean clothes to the living room and got to folding. I don't like folding clothes, no one really does, but as my hands worked on one task, my brain worked on another.

Someone in my family was a murderer.

And the house might be...reacting to that murder.

No one had used the H word yet. Not me, Christian, or the Miles family, but there was something undeniably weird happening. The shadow I assumed to be a detective, the blood showers... the doors. All of it was so real, unlike the films and stories. No lurking shadows that disappeared when we turned around. No rocking chairs moving on their own.

All the best ghost stories were when the spirits were let in by an unwitting host. A foolish protagonist invited evil into their lives out of desperation. Their need to connect with a lost loved one driving them forward in a traumatizing life lesson that somehow helped them accept their loss in the end.

But this wasn't like the movies. Whatever inhabited *my* family home knocked down doors and terrorized good families for no apparent reason.

As much as I hated laundry, there was something aesthetically pleasing by the way everything was separated and neatly folded on the coffee table. Creased edges of Christian's shirts folded and stacked, creating a linen set of folders. I got good at folding clothes after working for six months at Old Navy. I tried for Anne Taylor in hopes for an employee discount but no matter how many times I washed my interview clothes they still stunk of cigarettes and mold. Thanks, Mom.

I had no reason to be bitter. If Anne Taylor hadn't shooed me out the door, I would've never gotten the job at the firm. It paid more and I got weekends off. There's a difference between opportunities and happy accidents, though. Opportunities are things you discover and take advantage of. You see a possibility and seize it and make it your own.

Happy accidents are the events that happen to you. When life should've tossed you a lemon, but an apple smacked you on the head because you were expecting a lemon in an apple grove. Amid the rows and rows of possibilities, you found the lowest hanging fruit and called it a good thing.

My whole life was a series of happy accidents apart from the choices my grandparents made on my behalf. When their party hard youngest daughter came home pregnant, my grandparents strived to make my world a wonderful place. Even from her studio apartment in the senior living, she used what little retirement she had to buy me school clothes and supplies.

Despite my mother's tweaker boyfriends rotating in and out of our lives, Grandma always found a way to make me appear like any other kid. It was only on the inside that I felt wrong. Like if teachers and students pulled back the layers of my nicely ironed and clean clothes kept at her apartment for safety, they'd see just how dirty I was.

There were rules on how long I could stay at Grandma's senior apartment. So, while I couldn't live there all the time, I spent my weekends and several weekdays keeping out of sight. We'd watch old movies from her massive collection of VHSes. She'd tell me her stories and I'd tell her mine.

On the days she drove me to school in her massive Buick, I was clean and loved. Fully supported by the tiny old lady peering above the steering wheel, making sure I got into the school okay. Secure and assured on the days she picked me up. Her car would always be there. Grandma was never late, and she never forgot.

Christian came through the door. He stopped short of the vinyl border that separated the living room from the entry way. Staring at the laundry, he sighed. "What happened?"

"The detective called. Apparently, the skull was there since the eighties and now they want to talk to Gail."

He winced at that, knowing full well that Gail wanted nothing to do with my obsession over the farm. She had warned me many times not to bother with that place. It was on septic, relying on well water. The silo in the middle of the property was an eyesore and can't be torn down. The cost of tearing down the dilapidated dairy facility wasn't worth the hours. Not when there are perfectly good houses and properties in neighboring counties that not only cost less, but had less taxes.

All these things were true, but I just had to go back.

"So now you have to tell Gail."

I nodded. Eying the laundry, I contemplated knocking them off the table and starting all over again. That's when Christian went into the kitchen. I could hear liquid courage being poured into a glass without reservation.

"This is something you need to do," he said, extending the glass of red wine to my shaky grasp.

I sipped the wine. It was bitter and it felt like my tongue streaked across a chalk board. The sting reached my jaw before a soft warmth ignited along the back of my spine. Just enough that I could speak more freely, but not enough that my tongue did that sloppy drunk thing.

The phone rang on repeat without an answer.

"Well, she's busy, I'll just—"

Gail's full face appeared on the glowing screen. Dammit, she called me back.

"Hey Gail," I said with a smile, hoping it made me sound cheery.

"What's up, kiddo?"

Just have to inform you that there are dead bodies in the house and now the detectives want to talk to you.

"Well, it's a funny story, but...you know how you said I shouldn't go to the farm?"

"And you did it anyway."

Another sip of wine and the tension between my brows eased. "Well, Christian does construction, and it was a job."

"Oh, are they finally condemning that place?"

Anger threatened to ignite, but the flint wheel didn't create a large enough spark. "No, he was doing a few things around the house...that's not important. What is important is that he found something."

"Whatever junk you found from us as kids, you can just go ahead and throw it in the trash," Gail said.

Click, click, spark! I had to set my glass down for this. "What was so awful about having good parents, siblings, and pets that you have to pretend your life there didn't exist?"

"Mindy—"

"No, I want to know. What did your parents ever do to make you hate them so much? Was it because they couldn't afford to pay your way entirely through college? Or because you had to wear homemade dresses as a child? What?"

"I love Mom more than anything," Gail said. "But that doesn't mean I have fond memories in that house. It wasn't easy growing up a poor farm kid. Dad was sick and in a lot of pain. He took it out on all of us. It wasn't the life Mom has built up in your head over the years."

Cognitive Dissonance is a bitch. Even when I didn't ask for it, my brain was drawing battle lines and digging trenches to harbor my own versions of things. Christian put a hand on my knee just to let me know he was there. I nodded to let him know I was okay.

"How sick was he?" I asked. "What kind of sick?"

"He hurt his back in a tractor accident and was practically chairbound until they fused some of his vertebrae. After that he was the dad we knew and loved again, but for most of our childhood he was awful. Said a lot of mean things to Mom and even worse to Steven."

"Was that during the eighties?" I asked.

"No, we were kids in the sixties and seventies."

"But he couldn't, like, decapitate someone and build a secret place to hide the body, right?"

That wasn't how I wanted it to come out, but that's how it happened. The dropped silence on Gail's end suggested she was trying to work it out or maybe she fainted, I didn't know. Not that I'd blame her. It's not every day you find out that someone in your family is or was a murderer.

"Hold on... You found a body?"

"No." My voice cracked, and my throat became so dry it felt like kindling. "Not a body. Just a skull, actually. It was in the cutaway of your bedroom closet. Underneath a trap door. Forensics dated it to the eighties and now detectives want to talk to you."

"Are they sure?"

She had just learned this information, so I could appreciate the bewilderment. This only confirmed to me that nothing to Gail's knowledge had happened. Grandpa would've been unable to murder anyone in the state she described. This all might have been some horrible misunderstanding.

"Yeah. It definitely died in the eighties," I said. "A previous owner might have put it in there."

"My first thought was that Steven stole it from the science lab and was working on a prank."

I couldn't say. I knew nothing about my uncle. "So, they want to talk to you to get a sense of the home during that time. Make sure there are no suspects or whatever."

"I seriously doubt that." Gail said with a shaky laugh. "We were in our twenties, finishing up school. In and out of the house all the time. Dad was recovering from surgery, and Mom was taking care of everything like she always did."

I smiled at the mention of Grandma. I could understand Gail having unhappy memories because Grandpa wasn't himself. I could forgive that. It wasn't his fault he was hurting but it wasn't theirs either.

More than anything, I needed the confirmation from Gail that Grandpa couldn't have been the killer. Whoever bought the house must've used the hinges left over in his workshop to build the trap door. It's safe to assume that any buyer willing to buy an old farmhouse knew a thing or two about maintenance and building.

The police still hadn't found the rest of the body, which meant the culprit must have kept the skull as a souvenir.

"Christian, we're going to need more wine."

13

FRAGILE THINGS

"What an utter shit show," Christian said as he sunk into bed beside me. "I'm sorry you had to do that."

He sounded tired. I rubbed his back, searching for unyielding lumps and tense muscles. "I'm not. Whatever happened to that person didn't happen in the house. It's not our problem, and you feel like a giant ball of stress."

"Yeah, I got this new project manager who lines up my work a bit too efficiently."

I paused my massage and felt him squirm against my hands, so I resumed. "Should I add more time in contracts or maybe in between?"

"I don't know," he admitted. "How's the financial part looking?"

We hadn't exactly had time to discuss it let alone look at the numbers. I just assumed it would come up naturally but when he came home, it turned out that neither of us were up for it after six.

"How about every Friday we go on a lunch date and go over the week's progress?"

"A date sounds good. We haven't had one in a long time."

"Oh," I teased. "And it just so happens Friday is tomorrow."

He hesitated and turned to glance at me. "Tomorrow is Tuesday."

"Close enough."

"You're the boss…"

The next afternoon Christian and I found a Mexican restaurant near his worksite. I met him there and had a lime topped beer collecting condensation when he sat across from me in the booth. "This is a nice change from sandwiches."

Once, I tried to make an effort with those pre-prepped meal delivery services but between overtime and short notice emergencies at work, most of the food spoiled before we got around to using it.

"At the rate we're going, there's no reason we can't splurge weekly." I gave him the print outs from the programs at home. His eyes went wide at the numbers.

"Really?"

Really. I double checked at least five times before printing it. Even with an exaggerated amount set aside for taxes, the income from the last two months was more than we'd made in six. When I left my job, our bank account didn't suffer in the slightest.

"Come tax season I want to hire a professional, but yeah, you're doing it, babe."

"We're doing it."

I conceded the point and scooped some salsa out of the bowl with a tortilla. There were three new projects that required bids. Christian used one as a coaster for his beer but eyed the other two sporadically during lunch.

"What are you thinking?" I asked.

"This one is crap," he said, tapping the beer coaster. "I don't want to drive to Montana and live there for six months to build a house in the middle of nowhere. The other two are doable."

I had my reservations about the Montana bid as well but wanted him to make the call. "They will have to book later next year, though," I said. "I don't see you having the time."

"Oh, Robert is finishing up the roofing in Graham. I'm working on the others."

We were doing good, but two hires in a few months was a lot. Come spring, we might be able to hire someone with more experience. At this rate we'd need to.

"Does Robert intend to go back to work on the farm come spring?" I asked.

Christian stopped chewing and said, "It always goes back to the farm..."

I was stunned for a moment. He was angry. I could tell because he forgot to cover his mouth when he spoke.

"If he isn't working for you, we'll need to hire two people come spring and not just the one." My words were staggering and awkward. My gut felt like it was on simmer. I wasn't trying to talk about the farm, I really wasn't.

He closed his eyes for a long moment. "I'm sorry. I'll ask him what his plans are for spring."

Pretending that I was the wounded party in our brief skirmish was bad form. I had been high-key obsessing about the farm ever since he took me there in late September. His patience had been pushed to its limits and his typically placid surface was starting to ripple.

It was nearly Christmas. We typically didn't celebrate because it stirred up too many memories of prayers before dinner. Rituals his family performed on the eve of a stolen holiday. Just seeing Jesus being construed with Christmas brought on atypical rants about how Christ wasn't even born in December.

"I know we don't celebrate Christmas, but maybe we could take a little vacation."

"Might be our only chance. Come spring it's going to be really busy."

"And I'm sorry about being so obsessed with the farm," I said. "I wasn't thinking about it just now, but that doesn't mean it hasn't been on my mind constantly."

His blue eyes fixed on mine. They were sad like he saw something broken in me. Something he thought he could fix like a drywall patch or a lightbulb. But rather it was a crack in the foundation. Something far more insidious that required experts and relaying bad news.

"It's always been on your mind. I thought seeing it now would change that, but it's like you've never left."

Breathing through the spasm along my ribs, I nodded. He thought I was damaged. It was like betrayal and the feeling of someone being disappointed in you all wrapped up in one, sad analysis. My eyes started to tear up. The last thing I wanted was to cry at a restaurant.

Getting up from the booth, Christian tried to apologize. He reached out for me, but I dodged his grasp. He had a knack for simmering in resentment. Masking his true feelings until spilling the issue when I was least expecting it. This time, in public. I should've known my attachments to the farm bothered him more than he let on.

I was fighting with the lock on my car door when he came jogging out. "Wait, Mindy... I'm sorry."

"You're sorry I'm upset. Do you even get why?"

"Of course I do, I didn't mean for it to come out the way it did. I understand why you love that place. I just can't see it being a part of our future."

The car beeped and the doors finally unlocked. "That's not why I'm upset. I was trying to be on a date with you. Trying to ask about hiring in the spring. Maybe even talk about what kind of trip to take for Christmas."

Christian nodded. "I didn't know it was bothering me until it came out."

I didn't want to do this in a restaurant parking lot while a group of World War Two veterans watched the show. "I got to go. You can compile your list of resentments and hold them against me for months if you want, but I'm trying to make your dreams come true."

He winced hard enough that he had to look away. Good.

I left him there in the parking lot, and as he grew smaller, in the rearview mirror the heaving in my chest only intensified. I didn't know what to do. Part of me wanted to turn back, to say I was sorry and make up in front of the veterans. A darker, more wounded half wanted him to sit and suffer.

Of all people, Christian should've understood me.

I'm sure most people go through periods of their childhood where they feel unsafe, but I grew up only feeling safe with my grandparents. That house was the only place where I was impervious to the brackish stains my mother left in her wake. Even now, after everything, walking up to that farm felt like home.

Christian was the closest thing to that feeling I'd ever had, and I just left him at the Mazatlán.

I needed to collect my thoughts, and so did he. We seldom fought or stayed mad for long. He'd come home and we'd both admit we were wrong. Make up sex would ensue, and new life would grow in the wounds. Sometimes the only way to get to someone's heart is to carve through the flesh and break the bones that kept us out. Wounded and exhausted, we'd find a new understanding and accept it.

Just before I got on the freeway, a call popped up on my car screen. It was Amy.

"Hello?"

"Robert isn't answering his phone, and I didn't know who else to call."

Tossed from one strife to another, my edges were already frayed but the panic in her voice was a sudden shock, like I was being doused in gasoline. "What's wrong? Are the girls okay?"

"We can't find Charity..." Her voice was a pathetic whine like someone convinced of the worst.

Instead of taking the exit for home, I was already merging onto the freeway in their direction. "I'll be there in ten."

I promised Christian I wouldn't go back to the farm. We just had a fight about my unhealthy attachment to it. Yes, all those things were valid up until the moment Amy told me their child was missing.

The five-and-a-half-acre farm was surrounded by unsold lots. There were no fences to denote the end of the property. Just stakes with orange flags. While the equipment was sold off there were dozens of sheds, troughs, a ruined silo, feeding stations. That little girl could've been anywhere. What if she accidentally locked herself into the sick room or fell into the water trough?

My mind crawled through every nook and cranny of the farm, but even then, there were places new to me. There was a freaking trap door in a crawl space. What other horrors were installed after my family moved out?

The tires skidded in the gravel as I rolled to a stop. Lacy was sitting on the porch all by herself. Her little feet swung as she waited for someone to find her.

"Where's your mom and Paul?" I asked, pulling her into a hug. The poor thing was freezing.

"Paul is looking in the barns and Mommy is in the fields."

As much as I didn't want to do it, we needed backup. Still holding Lacy, I took out my phone and called Christian. He answered with a forlorn sort of "Hey," like he was about to get scolded again. We didn't have time for that.

"Amy's been trying to call Robert," I said. "Charity is missing."

"Missing?"

My eyes scanned the property. From the tips of the metal roofs to the rusted bar gates. "Paul and Amy have been searching for her for hours. I found Lacy sitting by herself on the porch."

The tremble in my voice was compounded by the damp chill and it gave Christian all he needed to know. "We'll get there as soon as we can."

Both were working on jobs in Graham. It would take them at least forty-five minutes to get here. "I'm calling the police."

I didn't know if Amy already had, but it wouldn't hurt to call them again. Charity was six and this was no place to be lost.

"Lacy," I said. "I'm going to run through the dairy facility to see if I can't find either Paul or Charity. I need you to be a big girl and stay right here on the porch. Can you do that?"

She nodded. Before I left, I took the extra cardigan out of the backseat and wrapped her in it. Lacy was already wearing a raincoat, but another layer might help keep her warm. Or at least be a comfort.

Winter in Washington meant the daylight lost its hold on the sky around four in the afternoon. It wasn't going to make searching any easier. I turned back to see Lacy still sitting on the porch under the light and it gave me some comfort to know she was safe at least.

One leg after the other, I slipped through the gate and turned on the flashlight setting on my phone. "Paul?" I called out. "Charity?"

An inhabited silence responded. Not like the eerie vacant quiet of an empty building where you're waiting for a pin to drop, this was full and alive. Organic and choosing avoidance. I was one of the myriad heartbeats on this land and with each scuffling footstep that beat quickened. Everything from the crickets to rats and bunnies froze as if the property itself was holding its breath.

A milking shed isn't a shed at all. It's a massive building with little in the way of construction or hiding. There are aisles of concrete marked by a sewage channel. Rows of iron bar stalls usually laid with hay for the cows to snack on while they wait their turn for milking. Cows go into their stall facing inward. They eat, get relieved of all the milk filling their utters, and then they go back out to pasture.

Without the cows, it just looked like a wide room with a jungle of bars. Cleaned many times over, it still smelled of hay and cow shit. They could take down the stalls, fill in the sewage channels and it could be a skating rink or an indoor sports area.

"Paul?" I shouted. The room didn't so much as echo.

Through the milking shed, there were smaller sheds. Rolling back the wooden slider, I peeked inside each, working from left to right. There were six in all. What were used for isolating sick cows or heifers who just gave birth were now used to store the hay bales used for the pumpkin patch. "Charity?"

There was no light apart from my phone, but I went in and scanned the first one. Oats and alfalfa flooded my nostrils. Not unpleasant out in the open, but when it was pressed into squares and stacked in a small space, it was like breathing in dead dry straw that already had me itching my arms.

As I left the shed, something scuttled through the scattered hay in the open shed behind me. Whirling around, aiming my light in the direction of the noise, I called out for Charity. Swallowing the saliva pooling in my throat, the smell of burning tobacco lingered amid the haybales.

14

LITTLE GIRL LOST

The concrete lip of the pool was slick with algae that continued in patches floating in the water. Brimming with rebellion and want, I was disappointed with the findings.

Grandma told me stories about a pool, but when I asked if I could swim in it, she said it was taken down. My child's mind wasn't so quick to believe what I didn't want to, so I waited until she fell asleep on the sofa and looked for myself.

I loved swimming. While other kids wanted to go skating I couldn't because my feet are weird. They point outward rather than forward which makes skating impossible. It's a concept people don't understand despite the obvious aerodynamics in motion.

She said they had to build a fence around the pool because the neighbor kids kept trying to swim in it. Naturally, I saw the bars that spanned from the milking shed to the back side of the barn and assumed that was the fence.

Clambering over the bars, I found the pool on the other side, just like she said. Just as I suspected. The pool was still there!

Grandma and Grandpa knew how much I wanted a pool, and they had one all along. Yet they didn't want to clean the pool. Why? And why put the pool in the middle of the yard where they once kept cows?

There were so many gates, and I wasn't allowed to wander in the dairy facility. It was like they set the pool here intentionally to be ignored.

I touched the lukewarm water and rippled the water and watched the bugs on the surface ride the waves as the fish scattered. Maybe it wasn't a pool, but it could've been if my grandparents cleaned it and built a ladder.

"Mindy Mounts!"

I winced at the warning tone of her voice. It was as if she were the farm itself. Every building and tree watched, daring me to disobey.

That was when I saw it. Gliding through the murky green water. Something scaled and massive. Like a shark, it soared through the water only to jerk into another direction. Picking up a loose stone, I threw it into the water and the primordial soup devoured it with a wet gulp.

Something broke the surface and for a moment I thought it might be a sea creature. Stumbling back, I turned tail, and ran back to the house before they came looking for me.

It was only much later that I accepted that the trough was not a pool. I just had to see it for myself.

What I saw in the trough itself were probably giant koi fish. Rather than flood their system with chemicals in the never-ending battle with rainwater, Grandpa threw in a bunch of fish that grew to the size of dogs.

My biggest fear was that Charity saw this trough and mistook it for the same thing. To find her floating face down in the grime. The air surrounding the trough had a fetid smell and the constant buzz of insects resonated in my brain.

"Charity?"

There was still no answer. Not from Paul or the missing girl. Amy was probably still marching through the overgrown grass in the neighboring fields and there were no blue and red lights to signal the arrival of the police. Where was everyone?

Something scratched across my foot. Startled, I kicked and flailed back just as the light reflected off a long tail disappearing from behind the trough. I grunted and shook off the pinpricks along my fingers. Rats were startling even when they were expected company.

The facility was one great loop that fed to the fields. Cows used to come in one way, drink before heading to their stalls for milking, and back out through the gated partition. I went to the fence and scanned the path with my flashlight. Reflective eyes blinked thoughtfully from a distance. I was being watched.

"Paul?"

The quiet was interrupted by a gurgling from behind. Bubbles erupted slowly through the congealing surface. Gripping the phone with both hands, I approached the pool. Holding my breath and preparing for the worst.

Please don't be a body. Not a small, child body limp and cold.

Pressing against the cold rim of the trough, I screamed her name again and again but there was no end to the bubbles. She might have been drowning at this very moment and I was just screaming like an idiot. The phone slipped from my hands as I pulled myself up and over the lip. It was like slipping into black gelatin. My feet found the floor as the water stagnated around my ribs. Shuttering from the cold, I waded to the center where the bubbles were slowing.

The floor gave way beneath my feet. A rush of freezing water made a muted, gulping noise over my head. I opened my mouth and screamed only to invite decades of putrid water into my mouth and throat. My sinuses stung as I flailed and kicked my way to the surface.

Something thin and ropey snagged my ankle. Flailing, I tried to escape but it only pulled me further. This couldn't be real. There was no hole to fall through but down, and down I went. Kicking and fighting to hold my breath rather than scream.

The world around me was black and something large and smooth grazed my side. The water gave way for me but when I lifted my head upward, the light of the surface was within arm's reach. It was right there...

I gasped for air and gagged as a clump of slime made its way down my throat. My feet found slick but solid concrete. As I surfaced, I inhaled just enough to vomit.

Shuddering thoughts of what I'd swallowed and how I nearly drowned cycled back into my mind and I gagged again. Retching a second time, the urge wouldn't abate because there was something gross lodged in my sinuses and dangled near my throat.

Stop it. There's no time for this.

Nothing I contributed to the water could make it more disgusting than it was, but more importantly, Charity wasn't here. There was no hole in the trough. Nothing for me to fall through. I must've slipped and panicked. Drowning in four feet of water wasn't going to do Charity any favors, so I got out and shivered my way back to the house.

Along with the glow of the porch light were reflective taillights of multiple cars. The police had arrived at some point, and I could see Christian's lean figure in a rainproof jacket standing by the door. He turned as I approached and came running.

"What the hell happened?" He demanded. "Are you okay?"

"Something moved in the trough, I thought she was in there..." I managed through chattering teeth.

He took off his coat and wrapped it around my shoulders and led me toward the light. "Have you found her?"

"Not yet." The temperance of his voice was faltering. Just as worried as me but trying his best to maintain composure. "I thought she mistook the trough for a pool like I did at her age."

"But she wasn't there?"

"Not in the trough, the milking shed or any of the smaller ones."

The police looked me up and down before one of them popped the trunk of their car and took out a heavy blanket. "Here you are, miss."

I thanked him and wrapped it around myself. "Amy or Paul?" I asked.

"Amy is inside with Lacy," Christian said. "We're going to comb the fields in a group."

Muddling over his words. Something occurred to me. "Paul must have found her, or he would've been back by now."

"We'll find them." Christian assured in that manly sort of bravado they did when they were too scared to admit they had no idea what to do. But I knew what to do. Jerking away, I threw the blanket on the back of a car and headed back into the darkness.

"Mindy!" Christian tried to stop me. "You're freezing and soaked—"

"Lacy said Paul went to check the facility but never came back. There's only one place left I didn't check."

At this, multiple police officers turned and began to follow. "There're several manure pits behind the milking shed. They dug deep, sometimes twelve feet down. If one of them didn't get filled, they would've covered it, but..."

"Show us where," a police officer said.

Okay, so I didn't know exactly where they were, I just knew it was a thing.

Cow poop had to go somewhere. The sewage channels in the milking shed led like railroad tracks down a slope that ended about fifty yards away into a bunch of weeds and bushes.

Police were intermittently calling for Paul and Charity as we went. The cold was catching up to me. A different sort of chill seemed to be creeping up on Christian as well. He'd been quiet ever since I led the police on what might've been a dead end. Maybe he was just scared. We all were, but the space between us was brittle.

There are so many silent agreements between spouses. The ones we don't say because to say them would shed light on dirty corners of our relationship. For some, it might be that one spouse needs to be the bread winner. Or another may one day want kids. The care of elderly parents might fall to one more than the other.

Christian had been accustomed to the fact that I had no family other than Gail, and like him, I didn't want kids. He was my home, but now he was competing with a property that wanted to gobble me up.

The core of his anger wasn't about the house, it was the feeling of infidelity. He wasn't trying to control me; he was trying to keep me. I wanted to hug him then. To tell him that I wasn't choosing the property over him. I just had something unfinished here.

A raw, muffled voice came from somewhere. It was slight, but my foot froze mid-step and I gripped Christian's arm. "Listen."

"Here! We're down here!"

The police surrounded a spot on the ground. We hung back while they ripped away the tangled overgrowth and revealed a wooden manhole cover. "Paul? Charity?"

"We're here!" Paul's voice got louder as the cover was pulled away.

They were on their radios. Soon more would arrive and both kids would be safe. I held my breath just long enough to hear the tiny sobs breaking and knew Charity was going to be okay. "I think we're done here," I told Christian.

We walked back to the house while the maelstrom of uniforms rushed past us. Christian remained silent most of the way. Was he really going to make me apologize first? I wanted to forgive him and wanted this tiff between us over but if he was going to keep this up maybe there was something deeper going on. Were there unseen cracks in our foundation?

If he wasn't willing to fight for me, what else could I do?

"Are you really that upset with me?"

There was a double take before he stopped in the middle of the driveway. "How did they fall in?"

Maybe I misread the situation. I assumed this had to do with the argument earlier. "I don't know..."

"That cover was secured," he said, whirling around to scowl in the direction of the pits. "Like it had been sealed over the top of them. You didn't hear them because of it."

A low, sinking in my gut wouldn't abate. He was right. That cover was too heavy for Charity to open. Someone might have left it open, but that didn't explain how Paul got down there.

"Christian, when I was looking for Charity, I got into the trough, and it was like a hole opened underneath my feet. And last time we were here, I was talking to someone. I thought it was a detective, but it wasn't."

"I found you talking to yourself on the porch," he admitted. "That's why I got so weird over this place. I thought maybe it was making you see things, but..."

I shook my head. "No, I am seeing things, but so is everyone else. Remember the cigarettes?"

He exhaled and fixed his gaze on the house. "So, what are we saying?"

I couldn't say it. Maybe I'm a coward. Afraid of being deemed mentally unstable like my mom. Only, she was unstable because she hotwired her brain with meth. It wasn't the same thing, but she used to talk about hearing spirits all the time. There's a huge difference between hearing inconvenient voices and something breaking down doors and trapping children in manure pits.

A swath of black figures rushed past us, I caught a glimpse of Paul's blond hair and the fury in his eyes. He was holding Charity like a father held a sick child as he rushed her through the emergency room.

He was furious and I imagined he had a story to tell.

"Call forensics," a policeman called on the radio. "We have more remains."

Bile sloshed in my stomach. Paul and Charity were trapped in a manure pit with a dead body for hours. The shiver from the cold became a tremble of rage. How dare it do this to them?

How dare it do this to me?

Another thought came swift and deadened the urge to scream at the night. They had found the rest of the body. That meant someone was killed on the property before I was born.

Denial is such a powerful thing. Despite knowing the facts, I still couldn't reconcile it. There had to be a mistake. Forensics wasn't a precise thing. It wasn't like they could pinpoint the person based on dental records. The murderer saw to that when he yanked out all the teeth in the skull.

Maybe it was better to not know.

"I didn't know you had a daughter..."

I didn't know why I was reminded of that, but I'm nothing if not a collection of memories. My own or otherwise.

The police were already questioning Paul when we stepped in the door. Amy was wiping Charity's face with a damp cloth to wipe off dirt. A stale tobacco smell ripped through the manure and fresh dirt.

"I'm telling you," Paul was shouting. "Someone covered the hole while I was down there. I heard her calling and climbed in—"

"Can you give us a description?" A policeman asked.

"It was an old man! Short guy, gray hair. He shuffled weird when he walked, but he was strong enough to pick up the cover and drop it on us," Paul said. His anger wavered between throat tensing mania and sobs. Poor kid, he was so scared, and the description was too similar to deny.

I had old pictures on my phone. Favorites stolen from photo albums in case I never saw them again. When Grandma died, I took as many as I could before Gail had the movers throw everything in a dumpster like she was disposing of evidence. I always resented her for that, but now I was skeptical. Why was she so intent on throwing it all away?

I pulled up a photo of Grandpa and I fishing in the creek. The muscles around my ribs ached because I already knew the answer.

"Was this the person?" I asked, holding the phone up to Paul.

His eyes were wide. Furious with all the indignation of a young man wronged. He looked at me with his bloodshot eyes and stood up. "That's him."

I swallowed and swallowed again to keep from crying but if I didn't let it go, I feared I'd drown. "That's my Grandpa," I said. "He's dead."

"He said we don't belong here," Charity's small voice cut through the confusion. "He wants us gone."

That's when I found the words that no one wanted. The truth we ignored was surfacing and being studied in a crime lab. The urge to come back to the farm was never my own. Something had been raking a path for me to follow and I did because I thought it was a possibility and not just a happy accident for once. What robbed the Miles family of their peace and brought me back to this place time and time again.

"We're being haunted."

15

LINGERS

P olice do not like unsolvable cases.

Despite Paul's confirmation, they insisted on returning with their own suspects from a database of locals with outstanding warrants. They couldn't comprehend what we were experiencing because it was beyond their jurisdiction. Above their paygrade. Out of the bounds.

"The more I pull away from this place, the more violent it gets," I muttered to Christian.

When I met the family and approved of their staying, the doors blew out. After promising I wouldn't return, this happened. The weird dream with Charity and the dog was a warning. Either from my subconscious or something else. What would've happened if I didn't come when Amy called? A cold sheen formed beneath my drying clothes.

As if reading my mind, Christian said, "It would've taken them days to find the kids if you didn't come."

It felt wrong to be glad in that moment, but I was brimming with it. All day I thought he was angry with me because he thought I was choosing the house over him but that wasn't it at all. Christian thought the property was doing something to me, and as usual, he wasn't wrong.

"You know," I said. "If a fire broke out, the Mileses would be able to collect insurance money."

He grinned at that. "Assuming they have insurance. Also, police these days are pretty good at determining arson. I don't think we'd get away with it."

"Yeah," I said with a sigh. Amy was rocking Charity in her arms with a feverish pace. They were terrified. We all were, but not in the same way the youngest Miles was. Her eyes stared vacantly with no signs of tiring like in my dream.

I hated this.

Being powerless in a situation sends trauma brains like my own into overdrive. I wanted to scramble and grapple with anything tangible to protect this family from my own. Just thinking about it, imagining Grandpa hurting anyone was like a thumbscrew to the heart. Why would he do this to them? To me?

The image of a massive fist slammed into a cow, right between the eyes. The heifer's eyes went wide with shock and rolled upward before she fell.

Gail threw away all the photo albums. Grandma never remarried. Once was enough.

"Okay, I think we need to have ourselves a family meeting," Robert said. The smell of fresh coffee wafted from the kitchen as we all sat around the table, except for Lacy and Charity who were put to bed.

Paul hadn't moved from the chair since the police brought him in. Still furious and tense, the muscles in his neck strained as if it were all he could do to keep from screaming.

I didn't know what to say. *I'm sorry Grandpa is haunting you...*

"Charity thinks this ghost — this boogeyman — doesn't want us to live here," Robert started.

"No shit," Paul clipped.

"Do you guys have anywhere you can go?" Christian asked. "Anywhere at all?"

It wasn't fair. This was supposed to be their home. Their peace. And my ghosts were wrecking it. "Maybe if I can speak with him," I said. "Tell him I want you to live here and that he needs to do...whatever."

"Do you want us to live here?" Amy asked.

I opened my mouth to answer, but Christian was quicker. "This thing has been going after her too. Since the night we found the skull."

I took his hand and squeezed. What did I do to deserve him? Most people would've seen that and thought I'd lost my mind. Given into hereditary disposition. But Christian believed me even when I couldn't.

"You've seen it too?" Paul asked. There was a calmness in his voice then. Like someone opened up a door and let the light in.

"Yeah," I said. "I couldn't look directly at it, though—"

"You got dizzy when you tried," he finished.

All I could do was nod.

"It also left a memento," Christian said. "A whole pack of half-smoked cigarettes in her coat. It knew she hated the smell, and it was taunting her."

"When I was looking for Charity in the facility," I said. "I saw bubbles in the trough and thought it tried to drown me."

Robert and Amy both scanned me up and down as if realizing for the first time I was still partially damp and covered in sludge. I didn't blame them, there were bigger things at stake. The coffee warmed me to my bones and for a moment, I forgot my crotch was still damp.

"I'm sorry," Amy blurted. "I just didn't know what to think."

"It's okay. I thought I was losing my mind, so—"

"You told us your grandfather died in the house. A heart attack."

My nod was slow, and my eyes went to the coffee. "He had a massive heart attack. Grandma assured me he died in his sleep. The part I didn't mention was that it was my fault."

"You didn't give him a heart attack," Christian was quick to point out.

"No, but before he died, he pushed for an elective surgery. He was partially deaf. Something about calcium build up. Doctors didn't want to perform it because it was risky at his age. He couldn't hear me anymore even with the hearing aid, so that's why he wanted the surgery. Shortly after that, he died. On my birthday."

I'd never said it out loud before, but there it was.

If Grandpa didn't have the surgery, he might have lived longer; and now, he haunted me. It didn't take a medium to see he was an angry spirit. One that harbored resentment towards me and anyone who tried to inhabit the house he built with his own hands.

"I don't know if I like the idea of negotiating with the terrorist," Robert said. "But I'm not sure what else to do."

"Maybe we can try a spirit medium?" Amy offered.

I didn't like that idea. The last thing we needed was someone trying to profit from this situation when we had no way of knowing if their abilities were real. What if they assured us they knew how to interact with spirits and gave us bad advice?

"How does someone even go about vetting a psychic?" I asked.

"Probably the same way one decides on a shrink," Robert said.

A joke, but clearly, he didn't know a thing about either. Psychologists went to school, studied, learned about successful methods of treatment. It was hardly the same thing. There was always a hitch when making friends as an adult. They always appeared rational until you got to know them. Their personal hang-up and ignorance were bound to slip out eventually.

"Well, if enough people recommend one, it might be worth looking into," Amy said.

I didn't know if I could run with that. "But what if those people who recommend a medium are the type who just wanted to believe it."

"In contacting anyone else we run the risk of getting them hurt," Christian said. "They would need to know exactly what they're getting into."

"The last thing we need is another body," I said, hating that we had to consider it.

Christian leaned in closer and rubbed my back. He knew exactly what I was thinking. If my grandpa murdered someone in life, not much would stop him in death. What would even drive him to do such a thing? Not to mention how. He could barely walk and was mostly chairbound.

"So, Mindy wants to try to reason with her grandfather's ghost," Robert said. "Maybe we could try it, but if he tries anything—"

"I don't know if I'm comfortable with that," Christian said. "But if that's really what you want to do, I'll support you."

We were well beyond comfort. I wanted to know why he was haunting people. Who he killed and why. The man I knew wouldn't throw children in a hole and seal the top. Grandpa was not a boogeyman, but why did he want to be one in our eyes?

"I want answers," I said.

"In the meantime, we're going to stay in a motel for a few nights," Robert said, looking pointedly at Amy. "It won't be fancy, but it will be safe."

The urge to throw my coffee mug at him became too much and I had to lean into Christian. Paul had been guarding the rec room with a baseball bat for weeks and Amy looked like she hadn't slept in a year. Charity was in shock and poor Lacy– who knew where her mind was at. His disdain for psychologists would need to change, because his family was in dire need of therapy.

At least they would be somewhere safe for a time. That's what mattered.

Amy packed their bags, and we watched as they whisked the little girls into the running car as dawn filtered through the evergreens. Robert lingered to give us the spare keys.

"I wanted to thank you guys. Especially you, Mindy." His lashes were wet as he blinked back the tears. "I don't know what we would've done—"

Christian gave him a pat on the back. "Get yourself some rest."

Robert laughed. "I'm looking forward to a full night of sleep."

We watched them drive off before Christian laid down some ground rules. "We come here together and stay together."

"Sounds good to me."

"Any idea of how you want to do this?" he asked.

I figured the best place would be Grandpa's workshop. Next best place would be his bedroom. But that could wait. "I want to go home and take the longest shower of my life and a nap."

"And I have some on site inspections happening in Graham."

The ghost would need to wait for human necessities.

Along the drive home, I found myself wishing — maybe for the first time — that Mom was around. She wasn't the most reliable narrator even for her own stories, but there were shreds of unfiltered truth in them.

They all had similar themes that revolved around whatever boyfriend she had at the time and how she was helpless to do anything about whatever situation she found herself in. Most of the stories ended with my grandparents bailing her out and the boyfriend ended up being a cheater.

I didn't need to know which guy she was seeing or how he did her wrong, but knowing who was hanging around the farm in the eighties would be useful. If Grandpa wanted anyone dead, it would probably be one of her boyfriends.

Maybe the guy who insisted on driving mom's car before wrapping it around a pole. Or better yet, the one that kept picking magic mushrooms to sell. That probably wasn't it. A lot of people picked mushrooms in the fields. Grandpa wouldn't kill someone over mushrooms.

My theories had some mighty large holes.

None of her boyfriends were malicious. Just young and stupid. Man-children who wanted someone to fix them or a free place to live. Not worth a lifetime prison sentence.

After Mom died, I did go on a mission of sorts to find my father. My only lead was Gail who let out an exasperated sigh like I was asking her to clean up a random pile of dog shit in the yard. "I think his name was Marvin. The Navy was sending him to New Mexico. He proposed after dating your mom for three months."

"And Mom actually said no?"

Gail's ginger-gray eyebrows raised. "I was as shocked as you are."

Uncle Steven wasn't married to my knowledge, and there were no conversations around him other than him not calling Grandma enough. Gail married her high school sweetheart and he'd become a background noise to her phone calls ever since. So, the only person who would bring the drama was Mom.

I did know there was some tension around selling lots of land once the dairy was retired. Perhaps there was some kind of incident there. A property dispute?

Not that I was an expert on ghosts, but it seemed to me that this was an issue of territory. Maybe what drove my grandfather to kill someone had to do with the land, and his soul was now tied to it. Like a punishment.

It was the most viable lead I had. Looking up parcel numbers and talking to the neighbors might shed more light on what was happening at that time.

My bedroom was humid and smelled of the bergamot in Christian's soap. He was already in bed asleep, his blond hair still damp. After showering and brushing my teeth, I joined him for the morning nap.

As my head hit the pillow, I tried to remind myself that the Miles family were safe in a motel somewhere. That there was a lot of work that still had to get done that day, and that I probably wouldn't have to go near the farm for another few days.

But the sensation of that slimy lump of God knows what kept running down my esophagus, made it impossible to sleep.

16

DISSONANCE

K nocking on doors in old dairy country isn't like going door-to-door in the city. When most of us hear an unexpected knock at the door, we imagine it's someone selling us something. Home security systems, pest control, God. Whatever it is they're selling, we don't want it.

In most cases, answering the door to a stranger is an imposition. Affronted on our own doorstep yet there's the expectation that we must still be nice. They know where we live, after all. Christian and I moved into a complex that didn't allow door-to-door anything for this reason.

Yet here in dairy country, I found that this is not the case.

The first neighbor, the one just down the way from the farm, was a woman in her sixties in a floral housedress who answered the door with a Bible in her hands.

"Hi," I winced a smile. "So sorry to bother you, I used to live down the street and I have some questions about my grandparents. Maybe you knew them?"

"Oh," she almost seemed disappointed. "I thought you were one of those Mormon boys. Come on in."

I followed her in, thrown off by the easy welcome. She seated me in her living room in front of the massive TV playing repeats of *The Price is Right* before suddenly leaving the room. Hands between my knees, I endeavored to touch nothing until she returned with a plate of cookies and coffee.

"I like to give those boys a hard time," she said. "Jehovah's Witnesses, Mormons, Baptists. I invite them in and debate the good book. Lord knows they don't come to convert me; they're sent to go out and confirm that everything their church says about folks is true."

"I'm not here to preach or sell anything. I just have questions. Have you lived here long?"

The woman had to mull that one over so that must've been a yes. "Since seventy-one?"

Perfect. "So, you were familiar with my grandparents, The Mounts."

Her ashy brows raised at that. "Oh yes, I remember them."

"They're gone now, and I'm trying to piece together more about them. They're not talked about in the dairy museum at all and my only relatives live out of state now."

"They had four kids. Two of them had the sense to get away as soon as they could. The other girl, the youngest, she was always barreling up and down that road."

Something within me twisted. "I only knew about the three."

"One died as a baby," she explained. "I don't imagine they wanted to talk about it. A little boy. Poor thing got the flu. That's when they tried again for the last girl. What a bust that was."

Did Gail know or did she just fail to see how it was relevant? It explained why my grandparents were so determined to dote on Mom. The loss of a baby must've been horrific for my grandma. Every parent's worst nightmare is to lose a child. I didn't have to have children to know that.

As if the woman suddenly put it together, she stopped short, and her eyes went wide. "Oh, I'm sorry, I—"

"It's okay," I said, waving her off. "I'm looking for some honesty. My family's need to only talk about good things has put us in a predicament."

"The cops have been coming a lot lately. I read the news. Rumor has it they found parts of a person up there."

"Yeah, and I'm trying to help the police and find out who it could've been."

She nodded thoughtfully, but she was looking at me with different eyes. Softened face but her dishwater eyes narrowed with scrutiny. I knew this look. It was the same as most who put together that I didn't resemble my mother in the slightest.

Who was I, this person in her house, and did I carry any of my family's traits with me?

"Your grandmother was a saint," she started. "Never an unkind word from her mouth. Always so warm and welcoming. Beautiful, beautiful woman."

"I owe her everything," I agreed.

"Mr. Mounts was nice enough, but he really didn't like advice or help. My husband went over to check on the horse they had. It was all patchy and sickly looking. Old Mounts yelled and threw a fit, practically chased Vic off the property.

"Someone else must have been worried about the horse. One-night Mounts came over, pounding on our door, demanding to know why we called animal patrol on him. We didn't, but he decided it was our fault and never spoke to us again."

In my dream featuring Molly, Blue the pony was also there. He was sick like she described. His ribs were showing, and chunks of his hair were falling off. Like he was severely neglected. Grandma mentioned it a few times, I knew the story about animal welfare coming for the pony.

"He was a curly haired horse," I explained. "Animal welfare thought he had Cushing's or was sick, but he was just born that way."

"Your grandmother explained as much, that's why we didn't call animal control. But someone did and your grandfather was furious. I thought he was going to break down our door with the way he was banging."

A chill went up my spine then. He was fully capable of doing that if he wanted. All of this wasn't surprising at this point. Hearing the story from multiple accounts only cemented that whatever Grandma said was probably the truth, but it was all the things she didn't say that I needed to hear.

"Do you know if there was anyone he really hated? Enough to kill?"

At that, the neighbor shrugged. "He had a temper, but he never struck me as a violent man. He didn't strike his kids, nor did he ever lay a finger on his wife. He was territorial, but that was the way men were back then. I can't imagine him killing anyone."

He was territorial all right.

I thanked the neighbor for her time and walked back to my car. I parked along the side of the road with the intention of visiting several people but maybe one was enough. It's exhausting to unlearn what you know about your family.

Peeling back their layers felt like I was somehow exposing my own. No one had ever lied to me, but they also didn't tell me the truth, and in a way, that was just as bad because my new skin was unable to withstand the harsh environment.

Across the street, the farm was vacant. The house perched on the hilltop alone overlooking the barren orchards. It was no longer the place I knew. Not like the warm, safe feeling when I saw Grandma's Buick pulling into the school to pick me up on a sick day. Instead, the house took the form of a predatory bird, just waiting for a lone field mouse before launching to attack.

"What happened to you?" I whispered.

In the blink of an eye, I was standing in the doorway of the milking shed. Flinching, certain I was dreaming, I braced the sliding door and confirmed I wasn't. In an instant, the promise I made to Christian was shattered. It didn't matter that I had no memory of crossing the street. Things don't just happen around me. My actions weren't an accident that I was powerless to avoid.

I'm not my mother. I am not.

The ground beneath my feet was real and this was not a dream.

Something slid across the gravel, plastic and heavy towards the manure pit. A hunched shadow of a man dragging something behind him wrapped in a blue tarp. His forward forced gait propelling his heavy trunk forward. Even if I didn't recognize the broad hunched shoulders of a man no taller than five foot four, I knew the slippers.

Suede tan with an intricate sunburst star sewn on the top.

It was my grandfather, and he was dragging a body toward the pit. He was a shadow of his former self. The pictures I kept of him were from his younger years. The time he spent in the Navy during World War Two or the few wedding photos where Grandma stood beside him unsmiling.

"I rubbed my teeth to make sure they were white for the photos and my gums started bleeding! I was too afraid to smile."

As if the person in the tarp wanted to be known, an outstretched hand came flopping out. Knuckles scraping against the gravel. The knuckles were already swollen and bloody as if they'd already punched their way through something but lost.

Grandpa didn't have so much as a scratch. Not a single bruise on his brow. At this point in his life, he survived on blood thinners and aspirin. A hair's width of blood supply kept his heart going. Any altercation no matter how slight would've bruised. Even using a hammer would tinge his hands yellow green. The person he killed, they didn't see him coming, but then why were his knuckles so damaged?

I held my breath and braced myself against the cold.

"What are you trying to show me?" I asked him. With no guarantee that I was safe from this entity, I persisted. Entity or not, he's Grandpa. My grandpa. There wasn't a man less dangerous to me. Not even Christian.

"Why did you do this?" I pressed, trailing just feet from the body as we made our way down to the manure pits.

Of course he couldn't hear me. At this point in his life even the hearing aid didn't help. He hadn't had the surgery yet. I could scream inches from his face and Grandpa might receive a fraction of the words. My voice a soft whisper amid the shaggy evergreens.

"Who is he?" I bellowed. My throat splintered against the sharp intake of air. At this, Grandpa turned around and scanned the yard.

Boldened, I got closer. Right up to the shadowy person with the watery gray eyes. "Who is he?"

There. A flicker of recognition in his eyes. He couldn't see me, but he heard me. "Who is he!" My voice raised so high like my voice came from the sky itself and I began to tremble all over.

Grandpa bowed his head and eyed the body. "She had no choice."

Who had no choice? I spoke the first person who came to mind. The one who never claimed to have a choice. "Mom?"

Shit, he couldn't hear me. I had to scream it in his ear. I was five all over again, hounding him with the same stupid question. Where are my blocks? The ones you cut and painted in your workshop? You said they were drying but that was less than ten minutes ago and a placating nod won't cut it.

The enormous man cloaked in tarp wasn't mom. Maybe he was telling me she had done it? I almost laughed at the audacity. Mom would sooner let the world around her fall apart than raise a hand against even her most disgusting boyfriend. She never defended me. Never took my side when they pitched their fits, upset that a teenage girl outwitted them or dared challenge their candleflame egos.

"MOM?"

"Yeah," he said, distantly as if searching for the voice. "Mom. She loves you. We both do."

Okay, one more time. I inhaled and prepared to scream the next question. Who was he and why did you keep his skull in the house? Only, when I went to scream it, my stomach lurched instead of my diaphragm. With a violence reserved for questionable shrimp from a Caesar salad from a food truck, the contents came forcing out as I spewed along the side of my car.

My knees knocked so hard against the side of my Outback I had to lean against the car as another volley lunged from my throat. Dizzy and feverish, it took several panting breaths before I discovered that I wasn't at the farm. No tarp and no grandfather to drag it to the manure pits. I wasn't on the property at all.

Straightening, I wiped the snot and tears from my face. I had to leave. Get the fuck out of here. Yanking the car door open, I took one final glance at the house. The porch light was flipped on.

#

Christian sat on the sofa with a beer in his hand when I busted through the door. He stood up to greet me. His eyes narrow and tense with worry. "Where were you?"

I thought about what I'd say. Working and reworking the events and how to tell him without sounding absolutely insane—or like my mother. When my eyes locked with his I burst into tears. Lying was out of the question. Not that I had a knack for it anyhow. "I don't know how, but I was there, and he was there... He did it. He killed someone."

"Slow down," Christian had me in his arms as he led me to the sofa. Collapsing against him I sobbed for I don't know how long.

"I went to the neighbors," I explained. "I wanted to hear from other people about my Grandpa. One minute I was across the street and the next, I was at the milking shed."

I told him everything. Every detail I knew and even the ones I wasn't certain of.

"I promised I wouldn't go back there. I'm so sorry."

"Not sure this counts, Mindy."

"Don't do that," I said with a fervent shake of my head. "Don't make excuses for me. Don't justify it. I was there."

"Okay, so what? You want me to be mad at you?" he asked. "Sorry, I just don't think it's your fault. I'd tell you if it was."

"Nothing was ever her fault. Mom got herself into trouble and my grandpa had to kill someone because of it."

"I came home early."

Even in this state I noticed. "Why? I thought you had to do inspections."

"Those were taken care of, but the detective called me. He couldn't get a hold of you, now I know why."

Wriggling free of Christian's grasp, I sat up and checked my phone. The detective did call. He left a voicemail. "What did they find out?"

"They found a DNA match to a local who went missing years ago. Gail and your uncle are being called in for questioning."

For once, I didn't feel anything. Numb from the shock from the shock of talking to my dead Grandpa and barfing my brains out, but...good. More than a little petty, but I had been trying to maintain what little strands of connection our family had left while they pretended it didn't exist. This had more to do with them than it did me, and I couldn't keep carrying this on my own.

"I wonder what they'll have to say to the police."

"Gail won't be happy," Christian sang, inducing a smile on my face.

"They've been hiding so much from me, and I don't even know why. I know better than anyone the kinds of trouble my mom found herself in."

I had to live with her and her idiotic boyfriends half the time. The one drawing a paycheck from a false L&I claim would spend his days in the shed playing video games and his nights yelling in a meth-induced paranoia. Another guy refused to wear pants for whatever reason and would walk around the house in his underwear. His massive belly hanging over his tighty whities— weirdly, not the worst of them. And that one guy that spent every waking moment looking at porn.

Yet no matter how sloppy, questionable, or high, he got to establish all the rules. He became king of the trailer and Mom would run defense every time I questioned why the guy who didn't pay a damn thing got priority.

Growing up, I didn't *know* my mom was an addict. Born with a disease that went undiagnosed until she was in her thirties. The constant pain of a crippling illness had taken its toll in more ways than one. Shit, even I still make excuses for her. When it comes to addiction, there're always tells, I just didn't know them yet. One of the biggest tells that no one talks about is this: He who provides the drugs makes the rules.

"Do you still want to try talking to the ghost? You sort of did already."

I frowned at the prospect. It was out of the question that night. A headache already thrumming between my temples, the ache of dehydration burrowed into my marrow.

"Not tonight," I said. "And...I don't know, it was weird. It was Grandpa, but not the ghost."

"You don't think he's the ghost?"

Yes, but also, no? The creature that terrorized the property wasn't the man telling me that he loved me. That version of Grandpa was the kind, reassuring person I recognized, even if he had been towing a dead body to the manure pits.

"It was more like I was seeing a memory."

Christian nodded. How else can anyone respond to this sort of thing? I was frantic and confused, trying to make sense of it all. My husband still had the capacity to take it all in without having a meltdown or puking all over the side of the car. Twice.

"You're amazing," I reminded him. "In case I don't say it enough. I don't know where I'd be without you."

"You wouldn't have stepped foot on the property if I hadn't brought you."

Breaking through the numbness, his guilt came crashing through my sternum. "Don't say that. I would've wound up back there one way or another, only I'd be alone."

We had sex that night. Slow and riddled with tensions we couldn't resolve any other way. After wordlessly showering together, Christian and I went to bed and didn't speak another word until morning.

That night, my mind took me back to the farm once more. Standing in the driveway, I stared at the porch light. Immovable and constant like the silo, my mind remained active night after night to watch over the property while my body slept. And while I stood guard, the shadow of an owl perched on the roof, its talons large and glimmering in the moonlight.

17

PENANCE

Gail and Steven booked separate hotels and came on separate planes. Joined only by a single dinner at a nearby restaurant, all that remained of the Mounts family were strangers.

Even though I'd never met him, I recognized my uncle the moment he walked in the door. The bags under his eyes and the impish bone structure. His resemblance to Grandpa was so striking, I gasped and clamped my hand over my mouth. I stood as he scanned the dining area of the Irish style pub. Gail said he only liked "American food" and I took that to mean white people food. The Mounts family wore their Irish heritage like a badge of honor, so I found the closest pub.

My heart collapsed in on itself as Steven looked right through me. Of course he did. We'd never met before. No doubt he expected someone who resembled *her*. Mom's wild red hair and green eyes gained a reputation of their own in the area. While I had her petite frame, my blond hair and strong, boney face bore no recognition for him.

So, I waved until my uncle checked behind him to make sure I wasn't signaling anyone else before shambling over. Just like Grandpa, his gait was stiff around the ankles.

"Are you Mindy?" he asked.

"I am," I said. "Gail's running late."

At that, he made a terse chuckle as he sat in the study wooden chair. "Some things never change."

I tried to laugh but I just didn't have it in me, so I smiled against the strain. "You look just like him."

"I moved to Vermont so that people would stop saying that."

Gail's recollection of their childhood became an afterthought. I should have known better. "Sorry, I know things were rough growing up. Grandpa softened over the years."

"Maybe for you, and your mother too," Steven complained as he took a sip from his mug. Black coffee was sweeter than this man.

Before I could say something, I'd regret, Gail came bustling in. Always telling me about a new diet, I wasn't surprised to find her plumper than the pictures. Still, she dressed nicely and had short red hair with lipstick to match.

The siblings mirrored the other people dining in the restaurant: white and elderly and eating mashed potatoes with gravy. A trio of senior women with matching hairstyles shared a giant pretzel hanging off a wire stand.

"Well," she said sitting next to Steven. "We're all here now."

It was an imposition for them to come to Washington. I knew that, but I couldn't help but take their unhappy demeanors personally. For Gail maybe less so because she had a vacation property in Cle Elm, but she hadn't used it in years.

Might as well get down to brass tacks. "When do you guys meet with the detectives?" I asked.

"Noon tomorrow," Steven said. "Hopefully that will be the end of it for me."

"Steven moved out in the early eighties," Gail explained. "I don't even know why they made him come all the way over for this."

"Kim's bullshit follows even from the grave," Steven said.

It was like I didn't even exist in their minds. Why did I even ask them to meet? They hated Mom, hated Grandpa, and by default they hated me. I went to all this trouble to schedule a late lunch in the only place in town that served schnitzel and they wanted to be anywhere else besides across from me.

Gail must've noticed whatever expression I wore and said, "Ignore Steven. He's an asshole on his best days."

"I am," he admitted without apology.

"So, we all know this has to do with Mom, but who do you think it is?"

There was a weird, silent exchange between the siblings. Despite not seeing one another in years, they had an entire conversation within mere moments. Steven gave a nod, which prompted Gail to speak.

"Mom made us promise not to tell you, but she's gone now and so is Kim. Given the situation, you deserve to know."

The waitress made her way to the table, but one menacing look from Steven and she promptly veered to another table. My heart began to stammer like I was being pulled into the manager's office. I didn't do anything wrong.

"Your sperm donor, Marv, was a bad one. When Kim told him, he tried to force her into getting an abortion. Planned Parenthood figured it out and helped her sneak out the back, but it got ugly."

My mind blanked with shock. Like the world just blipped off and back on again. Even ghosts were less surprising. Not because Mom dated a bad guy, that wasn't news worthy, but because no one else told me.

So, all this time, everyone lied to me? My whole family was in on this secret and safeguarding it from me. A lifetime of effort went into this long-running lie and it's not like it spared me from anything. I just—why would they do this to me? What did I do to deserve it?

"When Planned Parenthood refused," Steven went on. "Marv tried other ways. Spiking her drinks and even threw her down a flight of stairs."

"Why would she keep going back to him?" I asked.

As soon as it came out of my mouth, I knew how stupid it sounded. I often mocked people for asking such questions. Why did abuse victims go back to their abusers? Many didn't have another option. Conditioned and trained by their abusers, a person's mind is shaped to believe they deserve it.

"Kim was afraid he'd keep coming to the house," Gail said. "That he'd hurt our parents. With Dad still on the mend and Mom being the person she was... I think he threatened them, and Kim believed it."

I took a deep breath and tried to digest the truth of it all. The three senior women had gone, leaving just bits and pieces of their pretzel. Our waitress scouted our table just waiting for us to order food. Otherwise, no one else inhabited the restaurant.

Compared to my sperm donor, as Gail called him, the rest of Mom's boyfriends were saints. Sure, they weren't great as far as people went, but they never hurt me. They never lashed out with violent or verbal assaults. Some were better at manipulating than others, but the men forced into my life were mostly useless.

As a woman looking objectively at my childhood, there were worse things a man could do to a little girl. I would've considered myself lucky except I know that downplaying trauma does not lessen it. We were still impoverished and while a multitude of opportunities came Mom's way, she always managed to squander them.

"Why keep all this from me?" I asked.

Steven's rough visage softened all of a sudden. "You don't look a thing like Kim, but you sound like her."

"Your voice," Gail clarified. "Sometimes when we talk on the phone, I forget that you're my niece and not my sister. Mom didn't want you to know about your father. She wanted you to grow up as normally as possible."

That did sound like Grandma.

Even after all these years, Grandma still tried to shield me. I twinged of a sob racked in my chest. Don't cry in front of these people.

"We miss her too," Gail said, reaching across the table to hold my hand.

"She asked so little of us," Steven added. "It was the least we could do. Keep an awful secret from a wonderful girl. She was so proud of you, you know. Always talked about you."

I bit my lip and nodded. If I pressed my teeth any harder it would bleed, but I'd rather bleed than cry. I didn't know Grandma told Steven about me.

"You're all the best parts of Kim, and maybe the sperm donor. We just didn't want to take that away from you."

"So, all this time you knew Grandpa killed him?" I asked. "That could make you accomplices—"

"No." Gail interjected. "We didn't know that part. Mom said he left town after putting Kim in the hospital. That Kim would press charges if he didn't. He'd never need to pay child support just so long as he never came back."

"I still don't believe it," Steven said. "The man could barely walk without spending the next three days in bed. I'm surprised he didn't keel over right then and there."

I'd need to talk to the detectives. Confirm my DNA and that of the body matched. If it really was my father's remains, I wanted to know. The story shed light on the motive but didn't explain the decapitation or the trophy aspect. Why keep his head?

"Marv ran with bad guys. Biker gangs and such," Gail said. "Must have pissed off the wrong person and they left the body as a gift to your mom."

"If we don't order something, that waitress is liable to come and kick us out," Steven said, picking up the menu for the first time. "Schnitzel looks good. You seldom see American restaurants these days."

Their speculation was underlined with denial. As tumultuous as they claimed their childhood to be, neither thought Grandpa could be a murderer. He might have railed at them in the heights of his pain and criticized his children within an inch of their lives, but there were no signs of physical abuse towards anyone.

"I only told him once, before we got married," Grandma once told me. "If he ever hit me or my children, we'd be gone."

Grandpa must've took those words seriously. Either that or he just wasn't that sort of man. I suspected the latter. Still, after witnessing him drag a body through the property, I was forced to come to terms with the possibility.

"Excuse me for a moment," I said, getting up before they could. Gail's eyes followed me worriedly. As if I'd crack under the weight of truth and go on a violent spree of my own. Learning about my father wouldn't reawaken some inner psychopath, but having my own history kept from me just might. So many times I asked for the truth in one way or another and she dodged it.

Throwing out all the photo albums. Avoiding conversations about the farm. All in an attempt to keep this from me. It came back to bite us all in the ass.

Shoving the bathroom door open I braced myself at the sink. My fingernails chipped away at the cracks in the laminate. A sound like an exhale with a grunt pushed through my windpipe as a wave of dizziness took over. Fixed on the porcelain sink, my eyes scanned every imperfection.

They really thought this would all just go away, didn't they?

Like if they ignored it and lied, the bones would turn to dust and all would be forgotten. Instead, their little secret dragged them back to the place they hated. Why did they hate the farm so much? Grandpa being sick couldn't be the only reason. What else were they hiding?

I lifted my head and stared in the mirror. The woman looking back at me wasn't the pale butter blonde with saltwater eyes. She had a round face with long, flowing red hair straight as a leveler. I blinked and she blinked back before touching the nasty red scrape across one cheek.

She was dressed in a pink taffeta, some kind of formal dress. Vintage. Yanking the white satin sash with the words, "Miss Dairy" across it, she leaned into the mirror and snarled.

"I'm never going to be a poor farm girl again."

I leaned in to inspect the image, uncertain as to what played out before me. Grandma told me that Gail ran for the Miss Dairy beauty contest at one point, but she didn't go because she fell out of the car. Seatbelts weren't mandatory then, and in all the hurry she didn't shut the door all the way.

That's what Grandma told me, but the woman I saw before me had no intention of being Miss Dairy. I got the impression, like one does in a dream, that she flung herself out of the car intentionally rather than accept an award for her family's lifestyle.

A hand appeared and slapped her across the face. It hit with a resounding slap and I leapt backward. Her already dirty and wounded face reddening to a maroon hue.

"Never again," she said and slapped herself again. This time on the other side.

"Stop it!" I whispered. It didn't do any good. The slaps came hard and fast every time a tear threatened to form in her eyes, and she kept repeating the same words.

"Never..."

"...Going to be,"

"A poor farm girl..."

"Again!"

When the vision of Gail faded, my own, horrified reflection returned. With it came an understanding of my aunt and uncle's ire with their parents.

The very heart of Gail and Steven's loathing had less to do with my grandpa, and more to do with their occupation. Growing up, they must've struggled. They grew up impoverished. The animals had always been the first priority, after that it was Kim. Bullied for smelling like fertilizer while wearing second and third hand clothes, they resented my grandparents.

Deep down, I suspected that to be the case, but Gail always denied it. Kept the ugly truths a secret. Only, her memories came back to haunt me when they should've been haunting her. If they could see the things I saw, what the house wanted to show me, they'd know that secrets fester. It was only a matter of time before the infection spread.

18

THE HOOK

Questions about the paranormal came about as casually as asking how our day was or what the other wanted for dinner. While we brushed our teeth, Christian asked, "Do you think he even remembers who he was before he died?"

I stopped brushing. It would be easier if that were true. No longer Grandpa, just a fragment of him that resented things that happened in life. "Maybe," I said with as much thoughtfulness as one can have with a mouth full of toothpaste and saliva.

Since there wasn't a book or well-regarded expert, any information no matter the source was considered. Unfortunately, that meant the crevices of the internet were now about as viable a source as any. Some of those videos should've come with cautionary warnings or a pre-made tinfoil hat. Others appeared more legitimate, but if I had solid lighting and a good camera, I could've done much better.

"Do you want mustard on your sandwich?" I asked.

"According to YouTube," Christian said, from the sofa while I made dinner. "Poltergeists can haunt a person and not a specific location. Do we have stone ground?"

"Yeah."

With the jar almost nearly empty, I scraped just enough mustard for one. "Did they say how to make them go away?"

"I don't think anyone really knows how; they just sort of fizzle out."

Christian's frown suggested he didn't think this would simply go away no matter how badly we wished it would. If it was going to fizzle out, it should have by now. In theory, this thing had been haunting the farm ever since Grandpa died. It explained why Grandma moved out in a hurry and why the property went through so many hands. Or abandon state of the art equipment like the tractor.

"I keep having that dream."

"The one where you're just standing outside, and the porch light is on?"

Dreams can feel like they last for hours but they only take up a few minutes, but these were different. From the moment I fell asleep, I was there, and there I stayed until the alarm went off. The noises varied from night to night, hour to hour. Sometimes the peacocks would cry out in surprise. Mostly accompanied by the sound of crickets chirping only to all go silent at once as an intruder approached.

Coyotes would bark and howl in the distance and I'd watch the occasional pair of headlights pass by along the road. Yet despite the lack of action, I never felt bored. I never felt anything. Like I was in some kind of trance or a part of the property. A rooted tree, my legs were stiff and cemented into the earth.

There, I sat and watched. Waiting for something to happen but nothing ever did.

"It's almost like I'm guarding the house."

Christian slammed the fridge door a little too hard, giving way the torrential helplessness that came with being unable to protect your loved ones. We asked questions, but didn't receive an answer to any of them.

He'd been researching mediums on his phone when he thought I wasn't looking. I wasn't against the idea. Maybe someone out there was legit. If Christian brought it up, I'd trust whoever he went with, but so far just one page after another.

"Robert's getting eager to move back in," he said while we ate. "I think he's worried about the motel bill and the kids making too much noise."

"Five people in a room has to be frustrating."

Christian caught a drip of mayo before it fell on his shirt. "He said it's the best sleep they've had in months."

The letdown in that comment sunk so low. What if I couldn't get this figured out? They'd have to move. Without a down payment and terrible credit from letting go of that property, where would they go? Robert was already asking for advances on his paycheck — a thing that the firm didn't allow — took me all afternoon to figure out how to go about it on payroll.

"The detectives sent Steven home," I added. "But Gail has been told she needs to stay in the state."

Christian jerked his head in my direction. "They don't actually think she's a suspect?"

"I don't know." The detectives must've because she had a court order. I don't know what pissed her off more, the court order or all the cleaning that had to be done on the property in Cle Elm. "I'm hoping when the DNA is confirmed they'll let her go."

Not only were the Miles family depending on me, but the investigators kept Gail on the hook for whatever reason. All for something that happened nearly forty years ago. This wasn't my fault, and yet I couldn't shake the burden of it. All the pressure bearing down on me to perform a miracle without the facts.

With nothing left on the plates but crumbs, we had no more excuses.

"Are you ready for this?" Christian asked.

My mouth went dry and the residual taste of sandwich became sour across my teeth.

He asked like I had a choice. I supposed we could flee to Canada, but the dream would still follow. I had to resolve this. Not just for their sakes but for my own.

Christian managed to remind me why we decided against kids. His fingers tapped and thrummed on the steering wheel all the way to the property. Hyper-aware, he flinched at every vehicle that pulled out in front of us. A BMW cut us off along the road. Christian slammed on the breaks, jarring me forward.

"Fucking Christ, learn how to drive!" He screamed before laying on the horn.

Just imagine how nervous he'd be if we got pregnant. If I went into labor we wouldn't need to drive, just buzz all the way to the hospital on anxiety.

As responsible and guilty as I felt, Christian felt a weight of his own. Here he was, taking his wife to a place to consort with a malicious ghost. I told him I wanted this several times over, but I think he secretly hoped I'd ask him to call a medium instead.

The Miles family couldn't afford to hire a medium, let alone fly one out. I'm not about to pay for someone to wave some burning sage and tell us all our troubles were over. A priest might do it for free, but would that even help? My grandparents weren't religious people so I doubted Grandpa's ghost would even respond to one. Did it even work like that?

"Remember the time you tried to explain Lent to me?"

His eyes were scanning the road with hawk-like intensity, but a smile formed along his lips. "I don't know, I think you were okay with Lent, it was the Eucharist you didn't understand."

"Is that when you eat crackers and drink wine pretending it's blood and flesh?"

Christian nodded. "Lent is when you give up something for a few months."

"And rub ash on your face?"

"That's only at the start of Lent."

I could only shrug. At least it made more sense than Santa Claus. A fat man breaking into your house to give you gifts, even if you didn't have a chimney. Flying around on tick-riddled animals. The whole thing was so weird that when the extended family tried to roll with it, Grandma instructed me to always say thank you regardless.

"Do I say thank you to Santa Claus or to the person who claimed they're Santa Claus?"

At least I knew it wasn't Santa Claws because Gail married into a German family who pronounced it like Klaus. So, the visual of the fat man breaking into the house didn't include claws.

"That's fine," Grandma said.

"But what if I don't know who gave the gift?"

"You can just say thanks out loud. I'll send them a card later."

Another thing about Grandma. Everyone got cards. From birthdays to anniversaries, graduations, and condolences, she kept record of everyone in her little black book. Sometimes there would be divorces and she'd have to scratch out a wedding anniversary, but she'd still send my cousin's ex-spouses birthday and Christmas cards. I think she always wanted our family to be larger, but instead of nagging Gail for more kids or for Steven to have kids at all, she just made the best out of what she had.

I always loved that about her.

When I told her we didn't want kids, she said, "Good for you!" and left it at that. Not all my friends had the same experience.

And she loved Christian.

They met for the first time on Thanksgiving morning. I had promised to help her make dinner, but I got sick. Young and stupid, and thought I could cure a urinary tract infection by drinking a bunch of energy drinks. Instead, the infection went to my kidneys.

Unable to walk, in the throes of a fever and hallucinations, nineteen-year-old Christian carried me into the emergency room for super antibiotics.

So, I stayed in Grandma's bed while he helped her with the holiday meal. Gail still lived in Washington then. When she and her brood came through the door asking who the random teenager was presenting the tray of deviled eggs, Grandma said, "That's my grandson."

I can't say it went over well.

Being Kim's daughter, no one knew how I'd turn out. Gail admitted she held her breath and braced for another Kim-tastophe as they called it, but eventually Christian won them all over. I didn't understand it then, but considering recent revelations, I got why they worried.

I spent my teenage and young adult years feeling scorned by the rest of the family. Always interpreting the family's reservations for jealousy. It's not easy being the favorite, after all. Steven and Gail worked on the farm and received nothing but criticism as payment. They wore homemade clothes and were expected to pay their own way through college, but mom was different. Not that she attended college very long, but I could see where my aunt and uncle's ire came from.

The age gap of ten years made a difference too. Mom barely recalled using the outhouse or the times my Grandparents struggled the most. Gone were the days of selling a cow to visit a doctor or dentist.

There had to be some innate jealousy involved. Why favor Kim and her bastard daughter? They did everything right. Went to college, got married, carried on independently and successfully while I still clung to the only stable lifeline I had. The lifeline that should've been theirs.

If I were them, I'd be just as bitter.

But both Grandparents are gone now and there's no one left to barter with their ghosts. I could do that much for them at least.

Christian interrupted my thoughts with a wrought sigh. "We're here."

Anxiety swelled and festered in my gut. Which would it be this time? Half drowned in sludge or thrown into a manure pit? Fall through a trap and find myself face to face with yet another body? What if I asked it to go away and it didn't? Laugh in my face with some creepy, demonic laughter before it went off to do whatever it was ghosts did when they weren't terrorizing small children.

Charity and Lacy should've been off limits.

The man who raised me would've never gone after women, children, or animals. An unspoken rule among men of any decency. An obvious given that shouldn't have to be explained. Decency must've abandoned this property a long time ago.

"Okay," I said. "Let's see what happens."

When we arrived, the hill was cloaked in black. The porch light switched off, but it didn't stop me from staring at it all the same. We turned it off last time we were here, so I shouldn't have felt this... disappointed? The porch light was always on in my dreams. Seeing it off confirmed that I was awake and not astral projecting (thanks, Google).

Christian scowled at it but kept quiet and walked with me to the workshop. Pegboard walls held hundreds of exposed hooks used to house countless tools Grandpa had collected over the years. He picked up carpentry later in life. What started with just whittling became hand-carved trinkets, sculptures, and later furniture.

"Was this where he built the toy boxes?" Christian asked.

"Cradle and stools too."

At some point, it must've occurred to my grandfather that most of us would never grow tall enough to reach the cabinets. Even as a departure from the norm, I stood at five foot five. A gazelle by Mounts standards.

He built a step stool for Grandma and made three more after that. Same with the toyboxes and the cradles. And beautiful pieces at that. Newer furniture couldn't compare to anything he crafted. He preferred the Quaker style. Pieces that fit together without nails or screws. Precise cuts at specific angles like a jigsaw puzzle that all came together and stayed there.

Robert had seen the utilitarian room and hung up his own tools, but they barely took up the back wall. The worktable sat squarely in the middle of the room. The slab of wood that hung on the wall was no longer there. It said, "John's Shop". His handwriting was so seldom seen that something ached in me when the sign wasn't there.

At least that was something my family took with them. Steven must've taken the sign. A tribute to something they shared as father and son. Both liked to tinker. Grandpa taught his daughters how to fix plumbing leaks and change flat tires—anything two independent girls may need to know—but it was Steven who shared his love of building.

"I'd kill to see this shop in its glory days," Christian said with no small amount of longing.

"I used to run around in here while he worked. He didn't mind because I stayed out of the way and didn't touch anything."

A chipped block of wood still sat on the table. Pine and frayed at the edges. Something he might've given me to keep me occupied. My own little project to work on while he was repairing this thing or that.

If I touched it, would I be able to confirm it was mine? Could my fingers recognize the minute shapes and grooves of the wood, or my eyes once again find a distinctive ring that would've attracted me as a kid? Picking it up, gauging the weight of the block, I waited for a semblance of familiarity to come, but I got no sign worldly or otherwise.

Just a chipped block of wood.

"Maybe he won't come if I'm here," Christian said. "I'll step outside the door. Mindy, I love you."

"I love you too."

He closed the door behind him, leaving me alone. I walked, trying to remember which tool belonged where. Most of his table saws and things were over to the left. One wall consisted entirely of clamps, little metal knife things with wooden handles. Wood planes. A floor covered in sawdust from a multitude of projects. I closed my eyes and concentrated on those smells that my mind clung to, but only dust and cobwebs remained.

"Are you here?" I asked. "I need to talk to you."

No answer. And unlike the movies, there was no warning. No sudden chill in the air or hair rising. It's just there, and no level of preparation can stop you from freaking out, and then it's gone. If a conversation wasn't in the cards, maybe I needed to provoke it.

"I want you to leave the Miles family alone."

And still, nothing happened.

Emerging from the workshop, I caught Christian leaning against the wall, his body a lean shadow in the porch light. He was all shoulders and arms from his work. I should've known I'd marry a builder.

"Nothing," I said. "Let's try the bedroom."

Christian unlocked the house and flipped on the lights, but he stopped short of the bathroom just outside the master bedroom. "I'll hang back."

It wasn't just the notion that the ghost of my grandfather might've been shy. Christian didn't want to go into another couple's bedroom. Not that I blamed him. It felt like we were snooping. An invasion of privacy. We'd have to make eye contact with these people later. I'd tell them we were in there. They wouldn't mind, but it still felt weird. I wasn't transported through time or waxing nostalgic.

I was in Amy and Robert's bedroom, and it was weird.

"I know you're here," I said to the empty room. "Ignore me all you like, but the truth is, this isn't your house anymore."

Folding my arms across my chest, I sniffed sharply at the slight. Being ignored isn't something most enjoy. We came all the way here on a Friday night just to get ghosted by— well, a ghost. The least he could do was make some lights flicker.

Maybe Christian was right about the poltergeist thing. What if it was already gone in a poof of electromagnetic frequencies? Waves of energy fizzled out after a burst of activity leaving the house vacant. I guessed it would solve the haunting problem, but it did leave a lot unanswered. What was the point of causing so much terror only to spontaneously go away?

I left the room, my eyes connecting to Christians. "I don't know." My hands fell to my sides in defeat. "Nothing is happening."

"Well..." The muscles under his T-shirt went lax. Relief even if it did prolong the problem. I had to admit I too relaxed within the empty home, but at the same time it was frustrating. I came here to resolve things and instead I was greeted by an empty home.

"I guess we should just lock up and tell the family."

Already rummaging in his pants, Christian produced the set of keys. They jingled as he pulled them out. "I'll turn off all the lights," he said. "Meet you outside."

That was it then? So much for my big confrontation.

Simmering in disappointment, I watched as the porch light flicked off and Christian gave it one final glower before getting in the car. "I guess it doesn't want to talk," he said as the car thrummed to life. "Or maybe it left. Hell, I don't know."

Would it be too much to ask if a problem could just go away?

Pulling onto the main road, just before we passed the house, the porch light flicked back on. All the frustration went to my head. I didn't understand why he wouldn't talk to me. Why did he linger if it wasn't for me?

"It's taunting us," I cried, rubbing the tears from my face.

A hard, hallowed scream detonated from me then. "What do you want from me?"

19

***

FAMILY

L ife went on at an antagonizing pace.

Work was oblivious to our experiences. The foundations still needed to be poured and inspections still had to be conducted. Normalcy should've been a reprieve, but when there are no answers, it only feels like a hurdle. Like standing in a long line at the DMV while a circus act is swallowing flaming knives in the parking lot.

Eager to keep busy, Robert was more than happy to take up any extra work to extend his hours and it barely kept us on schedule. Another employee would've been helpful, but hiring for building in the wintertime was not feasible.

"I realize the work is delayed," I had to explain to an angry customer over the phone. "But we did explain that concrete takes longer to dry when it's rainy and cold."

"Can't you just spray something on it to make it dry faster? Put some heaters on?"

At least over the phone I could roll my eyes.

"I'm sorry, sir, but neither of those things are possible. We have someone checking the status of the foundation daily. Once it's dry, we can proceed."

Another call was coming through, one complaint after another. While the rain kept coming, Christian and Robert took to the indoor jobs. Mainly the apartment renovations we'd been chipping away at all winter.

"Hello?"

"It's Detective Rodrigo, got a minute?"

I straightened at my desk. "Sure, you found something?"

"The DNA results came in. You and our John Doe are a match."

My world tilted sideways for a moment as I tried to digest the news. My father wasn't some Navy guy stationed in New Mexico. He was a dead guy dismembered right under my feet as a child. How many times did I run and play just feet from where his skull sat, waiting to be discovered? It was so gross, and my skin went all clammy.

"He was my father."

"What did your mom tell you about him?"

"Just that he was in the Navy, and they lost contact when he deployed."

"Well, his name was Marvin Stephenson. His rap sheet extends six pages before the day he suddenly went missing. It seems no one asked questions because they were just glad he wasn't darkening their doorstep anymore."

Switching the phone from one hand to the other, I asked, "What was he into?"

"Little bit of everything. Theft, drugs, and assault, all before the age of twenty-four. He wasn't a good guy, Mrs. Lawson."

The detective sounded as though he were glad my dad was murdered. I guessed from his perspective it was better than a good person being dismembered and forgotten. Or the alternative of having someone like Marv weaving in and out of a system that did little to protect anyone.

Police had to be just as frustrated by the legal system. It did nothing to rehabilitate criminals and their records made it impossible to get jobs to keep them out of trouble. Armed with what little skills they had before they went to jail, a criminal had no choice but to march back out into the streets. Only, getting caught was no longer among the worst things that could happen.

"Do you want to see a picture of him?"

Maybe? I didn't know.

The curiosity was morbid, but it was there. I wanted to look at his face and determine if there was any resemblance. I also wanted to look upon the face that was so grievous my grandfather felt the need to remove his head.

Was it because Marv got my mom pregnant? I really couldn't see that being the issue. My mom was twenty-seven when she got pregnant with me. She would've been several years older than this guy and she always described her pregnancy as a miracle. Sometimes it felt like she loved being pregnant more than she loved the person I became.

"Yeah," I said. "I think I would. Are there any relatives?"

There was a sound of shuffling papers before he said, "A mother and maybe a sister? We can't seem to locate her either, though. Looks like the mother is in a nursing home. I'll send you the information I have."

I thanked him, even though it felt weird. He was still holding Gail in the state for further questioning, and I was just told that I had a whole other family that made no effort to contact me. So, thank you but fuck you? It's not like thanking a doctor for finding what could've been a tumor in a few years. More like, thanking your creditor for not sending you to collections for making the minimum payment.

After the ninth refresh, an email popped up.

The report uploaded slowly as my father's pixilated face formed sharp lines and hardened gray eyes. Semblance struck like a backhand.

His forehead and jaw were the testosterone-pumped version of my own. Tracing my face with my fingers, my touch confirmed what my eyes knew to be true. Marvin Stephenson was my father and my grandfather killed him.

With trembling hands, I took a picture of my screen and sent it to Christian. No words nor explanation. I didn't need one.

His only reply was, "Shit..."

Shit, indeed. The pieces were all starting to come together. I still couldn't imagine my Grandpa feeling the need to chop a man's head off, but the autopsy attached to the report gave more information.

"Unclean severance shattered vertebrae C4. Most likely decapitated by a large tool or possibly blunt force and decapitation after..."

My gag reflex was threatening to lurch if I continued to read. I had a lot of work to get done anyway. There were job projections and Christian had managed to receive two more bids on neighboring apartment complexes. They had seen the work he was doing for the competition and wanted a similar lift.

Christian came home earlier than usual.

Spinning around in my office chair, I beheld the beginnings of a storm. The rain pelted against the window and the clouds in the overcast sky were blackening. Sundown wasn't for another hour, but it was already dark enough to call it a day.

He sauntered into the office and plopped on the chair opposite of me. "So...that's your dad."

"Apparently I have a grandma in a nearby nursing home and maybe an aunt if anyone can find her."

His lips twitched at the information. "How're you feeling?"

"Well, my family lied to me my whole life and now I'm learning that they might've killed my dad."

As much as I wanted to defend Gail, there had to be a reason the detective didn't let her return home. A warrant to not leave the state took evidence. Probable cause. If she lied to me this long, what else was she hiding?

"Yeah, that can't feel great."

"I always knew, I think. Not the truth, but I always knew they weren't telling me everything. There was always this feeling...like walking into a room and everyone goes silent."

Looking back on my childhood, it was there. A lurking shadow when I smiled a certain way or if I said something they deemed uncharacteristic of what I'd been brought up with. The nervous exchanges when I was drawn to one thing when Mom always preferred the other. Any time I demonstrated attributes that didn't fall in line with her, it served as a reminder of something ugly. Something they didn't wish to observe.

"Mom had a temper on her. She'd fly into these rants, chew people up and spit them out. Grandma said it was the Irish in her, but I'm not like that."

"No, but it's terrifying when you're angry," Christian said.

"Yeah," I agreed. "Even when I'm furious. I maintain a calm, collected demeanor. Like the time I chased my mom's boyfriend around the house with a knife."

Christian threw his head back and laughed but stopped when he saw my face. "I'm sorry, I know it's not funny, but I wish I could've seen that."

I took great care to keep those tendencies under wraps. Each disapproving frown and nervous nod from those around me only confirmed that they were always afraid of me. Ready for the moment I might split at the seams and reveal the true creature underneath.

Treating someone like they're a loose cannon will only light the fuse.

But I wanted to be good. I wanted to be the person they loved and relied on even if I was angry. To be trusted that even my darkest tendencies wouldn't hurt the ones I loved the most. By withholding that trust, they pushed me away.

Instead, I pushed it down. Locked away whatever inclinations my family deemed unsavory. Anger, frustration, and paranoia no matter how warranted. If I exposed those parts of myself, my family would be liable to hide or tiptoe around me even more than they already did.

"In hindsight it was funny. I don't even remember what he said. I was chopping carrots one moment, and the next, a grown man was running away from me screaming like a little girl for Mom to stop me."

Christian was slapping his knee and howling with laughter. He'd always taken a certain delight in men receiving well-deserved consequences. "Fuck around and find out," was a graph and antagonizing women appeared to be right at the top of that chart.

I think it was because he secretly wished his mother had the capacity to leave his father, but religion is a different kind of abusive relationship.

He finally finished laughing. "Well, are we going to meet your grandmother?"

"I don't know that I'm willing to tell her who I am just yet, but I'd like to meet her."

"Keeping secrets of your own?"

"Just for now."

#

Not even five minutes away.

My grandmother had been under my nose all along. A pang of guilt came riding high through the nerves of meeting a stranger. Why guilt?

I didn't know I had another grandmother. It's not like I drove past her home only to be reminded of the woman wheeled out for the holidays. If I had any idea she was there, I would've cared enough to visit.

Christian stopped along the way to pick up some flowers from the grocery store. A small bouquet with some baby's breath and sunflowers.

The nursing home was an older building. Stick on squares of carpet and an assortment of chairs likely donated from closing businesses. Not a fancy place, few were in this area, but it was clean and the nurses in their purple and blue scrubs seemed nice enough.

"Don't think I don't see you miss Mary," a nurse with a large spiral perm said as she barreled down the hall.

"I was just going to—"

The nurse emerged from the hallway with a little old lady whose expression was that of a kid with their hand in the cookie jar. "I know exactly where you were going and he's busy right now getting his bath."

"Oh, well in that case I should wait." The old lady agreed.

The nurse did her best to keep it together while she escorted the lady away. She spotted us standing in the lobby and said, "I'll be right with you, folks."

Christian had to turn around and stare at a wall to keep from ungluing. I couldn't resist.

"That's going to be us in a few years."

His tone went soft then. "I can't wait."

I opened my mouth to respond but the nurse rounded the corner. "Thanks for waiting, how can I help?"

She guided us up the elevator to the second story. "I've never seen you two here before, Grace doesn't get a lot of visitors."

There were so many questions turning over and over in my mind. What if I didn't like this woman? Did she know I existed? Did she blame my family for what happened to her son? If she asked those questions, how would I answer?

"We didn't know we were related," Christian ran interference. "It was complicated between the parents."

"Complicated enough that a detective is involved?" The nurse asked.

Jarred away from my own thoughts, the nurse nodded. "Yeah, Detective Rodrigo stopped by recently as well."

"How much does she know?" I asked.

The nurse shrugged. "See for yourself."

Grace Stephenson's room was no larger than the apartment Grandma had after she left the farm. Unlike Grandma's apartment, there was no kitchen. I assumed there was a cafeteria or served meals. "How does she afford to live here?" I asked.

Social Security alone wasn't enough to pay for a studio, let alone a nursing home.

"Her husband's life insurance policy, then her daughter's."

So, my aunt was gone. "When did the daughter pass?" I asked quietly, not wanting to disturb the fragile woman sitting in front of the window.

"About six months after the policy took effect. They were forced to call it an accident, but no one believes that."

Both children died under suspicious circumstances. I was confident that Grandpa only killed the one. Maybe the siblings had too much in common. Both getting themselves into trouble and winding up dead. Their poor mother.

"Miss Grace," the nurse said. "We have visitors."

The woman turned, and smiled like I was the only person she wanted to see, and my heart felt like it was about to split in two. "Lydia!"

Her long silver-gray hair was worn in a single braid that hung to one side. Her forehead was wide and mostly smooth like mine. Was this how I was going to look when I got old? Also, who was Lydia?

"She thinks you're her daughter," the nurse whispered.

I approached her and sat on the blue loveseat beside her chair. "My name is Mindy," I said. "I'm your granddaughter."

Her pale ocean eyes focused, and she clasped a hand on mine. "I don't recall a granddaughter, but my mind isn't what it used to be."

"I only found out today," I said. "Marvin was my father."

"All this time and not once has he visited. You tell him he should be ashamed."

The nurse tried to warn me, she probably warned the detective too. Grace's mind was lost to time. One where both her children were alive. Maybe it was better that way. A mind might be elastic. Synaptic nerves can reroute when the way is lost, but a heart is a rigid muscle and only knows to keep on beating.

"He's been very busy," I said. "Never know where the job will take him."

She nodded. "The least he could do is call. Where did they send him this time? Last I heard, he was trying to get stationed in Italy."

"Maybe next year," I said. "He was sent to Japan instead. That's why he's had such a hard time calling."

I learned a few things from this conversation. The family resemblance was striking. She might have been senile, but I was willing to bet I looked just like Lydia. My dad was in fact in the Navy at some point. And most importantly, I learned that when it came to Marvin Stephenson, I lied too.

The last thing I wanted to do was agitate someone suffering from Alzheimer's, making the nurse's job that much harder, but there was more to it. She was so confident in her reality. So comfortable there that I couldn't bear to take that away. Even if she'd forget hours later, I didn't want to be that person who shredded her inner peace.

Who knew how these visits impacted the woman. She might forget mentally, but there was a subconscious layer that might be disrupted. Her days were forever impacted by something she couldn't recall or understand. It wasn't fair to her, and I wouldn't do that.

That's what Grandma tried to do for me.

It wasn't my fault my sperm donor was who he was, and who knew how that knowledge would affect me growing up. I wanted to be angry with the fact right up until I found myself doing the same for another. A lie to protect another isn't always a bad thing. Sometimes it's what's needed most, but it can't last forever.

My grandparents' secret no longer had a pulse, but the soul remained. Like a maggot in an apple, it burrowed to the core, leaving oxidation and bacteria in its wake. No matter how justifiable the murder of Marvin Stephenson was, it must've weighed heavy on Grandpa's soul.

Mom was always good with someone else picking up the pieces, but there's no way my grandfather would allow someone else to take the consequences of his actions. So, his burdened soul remained with that secret while my mother remained unfettered, as was tradition in my family.

On our way out, I spotted the bathroom tucked in the corner of the lobby. "I'll meet you in the car," I told Christian.

He saw the direction I was heading and said no more.

Bolting the door, I sat on the toilet and leaned my head against the tiled wall. I knew this visit would be emotionally draining, but not like this. It wasn't supposed to be like this.

I thought I'd gain something by meeting my father's family. A surprised welcome followed by an envelopment of people who'd understand and love me. They'd tell me all about myself in ways I didn't understand, and I'd feel whole in a new community. Instead, it was just another dead branch working its way to the root.

The home with the door always open and people who knew its welcome—such a simple ambition. For everyone else that was a natural progression, or they were just born into it. Not for me. The harder I tried to make my dream come true, the more terrifying it was for those around me.

I reached for the toilet paper to wipe the self-pity tears, but there was none. It was one of those canisters where extra rolls are tucked up inside. I reached up and felt it but couldn't quite reach. I slammed the canister with the palm of my hand, but the toilet paper didn't descend. Still, it felt good to hit something, even if it left a sting of metal against my skin.

So, I hit it again and again.

My mind went blank as I slammed the canister. Rage manifested physically in the usual tells. Heat rose from the back of my neck and my insides threatened to reach out and throttle the closest thing to me. The flesh and bone of my palm screamed at me to stop but I only flared against the pain and hit the canister so hard the screws jarred from the wall.

They didn't even tile behind the toilet paper dispenser. It was just sheetrock and they tiled around it. For some reason that pissed me off even more than the lock on the canister mocking me. I leaned in the opposite direction and kicked the dispenser. Even clanging to the floor, the toilet paper didn't come out. At least I was satisfied.

No one was in the lobby when I emerged. Most in this place were either deaf or senile anyhow. I was worried the nurse would come in and ask what was going on, but she was too busy caring for her charges.

Christian was singing along with the radio when I got in. "Are you okay?"

Fastening my seatbelt, I said, "Yeah, I think something disagreed with me."

"Hopefully it wasn't the eggs, I just bought those."

I checked my face in the side mirror for tells of what happened in the bathroom. I was paler than usual, but otherwise normal. No splotches or anything. My red and numb palm remained flat against my leg. Hopefully it didn't bruise.

Just as I went to look away, my reflection winked back at me as if assuring it was our little secret.

20

CABBAGE

When we parked the car, the first thing I noticed was that the porch light was off. Must've been a real power outage and not a haunted one. The light switch flipped but no light followed. There was a half-hearted flicker, but that was it.

"Sure," Christian breathed. "Why not?"

Even with the electricity out, the house thrummed with an undeniable energy. It wasn't like before, when someone else's memories were dredged from the deep or some manifestation appeared, this was like static. Every tiny hair rose and the top layer of my skin was charged.

"Can you feel it too?" I asked. It was either that or the alternative, I'd finally snapped.

"Yeah," Christian said, turning on the flashlight. "It's like walking along an electric fence. Constantly aware that it'll shock the shit out of you. Only, we don't know where the fence is."

That pretty much summed it up. What we were searching for was here on arrival, so all there was left to do was wait for it to surface and try to negotiate. I sat down at the table and Christian joined me. The legs of the chair skidded against the tile, and he winced at the sound that echoed. "Sorry."

"I don't think the ghosts mind."

"So, we're just going to wait this one out?"

"Mm hm."

"Cool..." he said, rubbing his hands together between his knees. "Cool."

I needed to distract him. There was no way he could sit in the dark room filled with kinetic energy and stay quiet. He was understandably nervous, but why wasn't I? If anything, I felt calmer than I had in weeks—months even. Like someone wrapped me in a plush blanket and handed me a hot toddy. I was warm and content even if I was afraid to touch any outlets.

"I know things have been weird," I said. "But I wanted you to know that I'm so proud of you. Your business has changed our lives for the better."

"Our business," Christian reminded. "I was up to my neck in paperwork until you came along. Now I'm actually efficient."

"Yeah, but now that I'm working with you, we're going to need two years' worth of taxes before we can even think of moving out of the apartment."

A discussion reserved for road trips and late nights in bed, buying our own home was the dream we reserved for the most intimate conversations. Being married is funny like that. When we dated, it was all about being whisked off our feet and what we'd do for secret rendezvous. These days, it was about what kind of home we'd like to settle in. Retirement. Indoor plants.

"I imagine all of this has changed your mind on where you'd like to live," he said.

Nodding, I glanced around the dark room. Had it? This place had always been my dream. The ability to come back here, to make it my own. The property itself was an investment of a lifetime but it did have its flaws.

"I don't think I want this place so much as I want a place that makes me feel the way I did when I lived here."

"You carry that with you wherever you go," Christian said, gently poking my heart.

It was so cliché it had to be true. "I always thought that the history here is what made me safe, but the more I learn the truth the more confusing it gets."

In my mind, this was a perfect world that I once existed in and was trying to come back to. Taken away by circumstance. Only, it wasn't perfect. Gail had tried to tell me as much, even the ghosts tried to warn me, but I couldn't deny the thrum of inner peace that still resided here.

"So, learning that your grandfather murdered your father and dumped him in a manure pit didn't frighten you?"

"It probably should've, but I'm more concerned about the current stakes. Gail and the Miles family."

"Okay."

His clipped response told me he didn't agree. "Oh, come on, like people haven't died in the houses you've worked on."

"Died, sure. Not murdered in some unsolved family saga. You aren't the least bit angry that your father was murdered?"

I probably should've been, but I wasn't.

"I just want to understand what led to it. Why is Gail still a suspect? Why is it still haunting us? Me I get, but not Charity. Not the family."

"You're more concerned about the tangible consequences, but what I'm concerned about are the moral implications. Murder is one of the worst sins, you don't have to believe in God to know that one. Aren't you worried that his soul is trapped here because of it?"

It was an awkward twist in logic for me. One I hadn't faced outright.

Christian was raised in a cult that worshiped a zombie-like figure and sheep herders that hallucinated around burning bushes. He was taught that murder — apart from a whole slew of exceptions — was wrong.

That wasn't the case for me. Death on a farm was a fact of life. Something that was necessary to stop the suffering or feed the hungry. Who knew how many living things died here? Marvin's death might've been unnatural, but I couldn't say it was wrong.

"Maybe," I said. "But I don't believe it's a punishment from a higher being so much as it's his own guilt and memories that keeps him here."

He nodded as if he had just realized something for the first time. "That's why you're so determined to fix it. You think your grandfather is trapped."

It had to be the reason I was so drawn to this place. Why it occupied most of my thoughts, waking or otherwise. There was unresolved business here and it had to do with me. Everything we'd learned thus far confirmed it. The truth was that I couldn't leave this place until this spirit did.

So here I sat, and despite it all, Christian sat beside me.

An unexpected sound came from the kitchen. I froze, disconcerted as I tried to figure out what it was. A soft, fleshy thud followed by a gentle roll. Christian heard it too and snatched his phone to aim it at the floor. What happened next could only be described as perplexing.

A large head of cabbage came rolling from around the corner. The produce rounded the kitchen peninsula before teetering back and forth a foot from the door. Like it had a life of its own, the vegetable took a casual stroll before pausing at the door as if hoping someone would be polite enough to see it out.

The light remained on the cabbage as if Christian expected it to grow legs and come running toward us, but this wasn't a haunted cabbage.

It was quite literally just a cabbage.

The air lessened then. Whether the tension in the room had evaporated or it wandered off like the vegetable, I erupted in laughter.

Christian was up and investigating the kitchen. "The fridge door is closed. Maybe it rolled off the counter? I think I would've remembered if the Mileses left a cabbage on the counter."

I shook my head, tears stinging my eyes as I laughed. How could I explain it if I couldn't stop laughing? My ribs were starting to ache. Christian's expression was the same as the time he came home to find me accidentally drunk on Schnapps.

"It's a memory," I said.

"Who's?"

I wasn't even sure anymore. Grandma told the story so many times I remembered it for myself, but it was years before I was born. Maybe even before my mom's time. "One of my grandparent's parties. They were all shitfaced when someone opened the fridge and a cabbage fell out. It did, well...that."

Christian wasn't laughing. He might've found it funny under different circumstances, or maybe he just had to be there. "So, that's it?"

"That's the whole story."

He aimed the light near the door only to find the cabbage had disappeared.

"That's enough for tonight," Christian said, hastily rushing me out the door.

"Flashbacks to your grocer days?"

"Mindy, shit is appearing and disappearing." His voice was almost as trembly as his hands.

"I'm sorry," I said, regaining some composure. "It's not funny. I just know it's a memory and not—"

"Memories reenact in your head, not your living room. And that's not even *your* memory."

I stopped laughing then. It wasn't my memory, but the house had chosen to show it to me. In doing so, the story became my own.

Christian was thinking so loud in the car ride home that I half expected him to start ranting or roll down the windows and start yelling about produce at the homeless camp parked by the stop sign.

"So, what we saw wasn't a ghost, it was a memory."

"I think so. Just like the one I experienced with Grandpa dragging Marv's body in a tarp."

Only, I was able to interact with him at some capacity. I left that part out because Christian was already struggling with this. He signed up for sickness and in health, til death do us part—not the stuff that might come after.

"But there's also a spirit."

"Yes, the thing that tossed the kids into the manure pit and spoke to me." Not to mention attempt to drown me. The doors being knocked off their hinges might've been a memory, but it wasn't one that I knew. Grandma never told me anything about it.

"How do you make memories stop?"

It was a question we both sat with like a drunk passenger in the back seat. If we spoke too loudly, they might wake and ask to pull over to puke for the third time.

Memories don't go away. Our recollection and understanding of them can shift. We can learn every facet of the moment burned into our minds and it might even alter what we see, but they never go away entirely.

"We need to get some help, Mindy." It wasn't a statement so much as a plea for help.

That was real world complicated. "Who's going to pay for it? Us or the Miles family?"

"At this rate I don't even care."

That meant we'd be paying for a medium for a house that didn't belong to us. Yes, I was clearly involved and being haunted as well, but it felt like picking up the tab for someone else's dinner. Not to mention...

"Shouldn't we clear this with them first? It's their house."

"Amy has been talking to someone for a while now. Miles told me."

Ah, it was a coup. Everyone had already decided on this, and Christian was holding off the medium until he could see with his own eyes that we were all in over our heads. It didn't feel particularly good being the one on the outside of a decision. Especially when I wasn't opposed to it so much as I was opposed to us paying for it.

It was one thing to help the family with my time and effort, but it was another to pay someone who probably didn't know what they were in for anymore than the rest of us.

"How much is it going to cost?"

"This woman is willing to come if we pay for travel. She lives in California, so not that much. The family will move back in, she'll stay with them."

I supposed they couldn't live in a motel forever.

"Okay, but they should have her sign something. To protect them from any liability."

Christian was nodding in firm agreement. The last thing anyone needed was a lawsuit.

Just another stranger traversing through my family history. What could go wrong?

21

— • —

Skin in the Game

The family moved back in with as much enthusiasm as a pig to the slaughterhouse.

Poor Charity had to be carried in while Lacy clung to Amy's leg. Paul followed behind as he scanned the perimeter waiting for the unexpected. I hated how afraid they were. The fact that the kids preferred the motel room to the farm was devastating.

The red dots that freckled every bit of exposed skin confirmed they had also taken bed mites in stride—just so long as they didn't have to go back. What could I do to help? There were no promises or assurances I could give. I'd hoped I could be the one to promise their home was safe, but I had to leave that to the frail bird of a woman emerging from Robert's truck.

Her hair was an ashy brown that frizzed rather than curled. She was beautiful in that older, natural way. No make-up or Botox, just clear skin that stretched taut over her prominent bones.

"You must be Mindy," the woman said. "I'm Lorraine."

Strangling the chuckle in my throat, I wondered if that was her real name. Perhaps it was a homage to Lorraine Warren. Where was her Ed? Still, I did expect more mysticism. She didn't wear funky jewelry found at the flea market. No crosses or anything. She wore ballet flats and a loose-fitting green shift dress capped with a knitted blue shawl.

"Nice to meet you," I said.

She turned to observe the house. "So, you grew up here and now it's haunted."

"And now it's haunted." It still felt weird saying that out loud.

"But not just ghosts...memories too?"

"Have you ever dealt with anything like that before?" I pressed.

Skepticism was something Lorraine must've received a lot of because she didn't hesitate in the slightest. "Nope. So, this will be new for me too."

Rocking on my heels, I watched Lorraine walk away, unable to deny the growing respect. In an occupation where she could make up anything, she told the truth. In a world where people padded their resumes only to sit down in the chair and google for answers, this woman admitted she didn't have them. It was oddly reassuring.

Trailing into the house, I leaned against the peninsula while Lorraine walked about in a slow, thoughtful manner. "When was the house built?"

"Fifty-two," I said.

She eyed the outlets and said, "Wouldn't be up to code these days."

"Not in the slightest," Christian agreed.

Paul watched the woman with an expression that suggested he wasn't buying any of it before joining me.

"How've things been?" I asked him.

"Shitty."

"I'm so sorry—"

"It's not your fault," Paul interrupted. "I don't know why he refuses to just short sell the place and leave. He went from not believing us to hiring this lady when they can barely afford to live here."

I didn't know what to say. He wasn't wrong, but I couldn't blame Robert for not wanting to leave when I was the same. I fantasized about owning this property even though I wasn't a farmer. I didn't even like the house. Not just the outdated interior. The overall layout was so inefficient I doubted Christian could even save it. What would I do with a three-bedroom house anyway?

Not that I wanted to live here anymore. I couldn't pay Christian to live here, not after the cabbage incident. But I could see why Robert was fixated on it. What could I tell Paul that would make sense? I didn't know his father's motivations, just the sentimentality of a fading dream. But for Robert it was still a possibility even if his family didn't agree. It could also be that Robert didn't want to return to Colorado a failed farmer. What did adults have if not pride?

Telling Paul he'd understand when he's older just sounded patronizing.

"I wish I could say adults know what we're doing, but the truth is, we don't. Especially when it comes to the things we can't explain."

Here I was, hurtling towards thirty and I still had to remind myself that I was an adult. Capable of making decisions and doing things without permission. Maybe that's why people clung to religion so readily. They needed an adult to speak to, a parental image to defy.

A cry broke out from the bathroom.

Paul and I both startled at the noise. The boy practically bolted for the bathroom but stopped shy of barging in. He leaned in and listened and sheepishly walked back. "Lacy is at a phase where she doesn't want to take baths."

The panic simmered down as Amy's voice could be heard reassuring Lacy that she needed a bath. Outside, Robert was leading Lorraine towards the milking shed. Safe from being overheard, I asked him, "Do you think she's the real deal?"

"Who knows." He wiped his long bangs from his face and peered out the window. "Maybe she will tell him it's a lost cause."

I was pretty sure the biggest reason Robert wanted to stay was because they couldn't afford to move. Not into an apartment or a new house. If he did a short sell, everything would go to the bank. They'd have nothing left. For whatever reason, Robert didn't want to explain that to Paul, so neither could I. It wasn't my business anyway.

"If she can get rid of the ghost, this place wouldn't be so bad," I offered.

"Yeah, right."

Sarcasm is one of the tools in a teenager's toolbelt, but I chaffed a little when he said that. I would've been thrilled if Grandma kept this place after Grandpa died. I know she couldn't because it was too expensive to keep and the property taxes were murder, but if given the option I would have stayed.

"So, what's your deal?" Paul asked. "Why are you still hanging around?"

At this point, he had a right to ask. "I don't know how much your parents have told you, but the body found on this property was my father's."

Paul's mouth drooped at that.

"My aunt is the only living suspect, so if I can prove she didn't kill him, she can go home to California."

That, and the ghosts were haunting me too. The porch light dreams continued no matter what I did, and when I woke the next morning, it felt like I hadn't slept. I tried sleeping pills, but all that did was make the dream happen faster. Telling Paul any of that felt too intimate.

Robert and Lorraine were walking back toward the house.

The kid and I both shuffled into seats around the dining room table, trying to act natural, like we weren't just spying on them.

When the door opened, Lorraine stepped inside and took off her soaked flats. "I wore the wrong shoes for this."

"Coffee?" Robert asked.

"Please," Lorraine said as she joined us at the table.

I squirmed in the seat while Robert took his time picking out the right mugs. Asking if we wanted sugar or creamer. Yelling to Amy to see if she too wanted some coffee. *Sit the hell down, Robert. I want to know what the lady has to say.*

Paul's lips quirked before he took out his phone and began scrolling.

Lorraine smiled as the cup was set before her. Robert finally sat down before the medium spoke. "Right away, I can tell you there is a presence, but you already know that. I'm betting there's more than just one, and I can tell you it all centers around a single nexus event."

"Nexus event?" Robert asked.

A strand of her hair fell into the coffee as she turned to regard him. "There are many types of hauntings. A nexus event is an incident so unnatural to a person's spirit that it traps them in that moment after death."

"What traumatized them in life traps them in death," Paul said.

Lorraine nodded. "In this case, we have a good idea what the nexus event is."

Of course they told her about the body. Why not just give every detail to make her job easier? Wanting to believe is a lot different than actual belief. When the car dealership hands me a pair of keys and says "congratulations", it's easy to believe I own the car. A woman with all the facts filling in the blanks with her own catch phrases sounds official, but it's hard to swallow.

"Then can you stop it?" Robert asked.

"So, a nexus event typically traps several spirits. It's like a spiderweb, all the souls involved get caught in it. By going through and untangling the souls from this event, the overall haunting will diminish. Even if I can't free the main spirit."

I straightened. "What if you can't free the main spirit? Does he just stay trapped here alone forever?"

Lorraine turned to face me then. "You suspect it's your grandfather. I wouldn't want my loved ones trapped in purgatory either. I'm going to try my best to free him."

It was that slinking feeling like when a doctor avoids answering until after they try treatment. They don't know the size of the tumor or if it's even operable, they just know based on the blood work and symptoms that it's fucking cancer because everything is cancer.

Still, I didn't like it. Her tone and explanation were too well-rehearsed to be genuine. Best practices applied but no skin in the game.

"But say you can't free every spirit, the overall outcome is less haunted," Robert concluded.

"The fewer the spirits, the less power the nexus event has, the less it makes itself known to our world," Lorraine said.

"How many times have you done this?" I asked.

"Hundreds," Lorraine confirmed. "It's one of the most common haunting types."

"What's the other?" Paul asked, peeking over his phone.

"Memories," Lorraine was looking at me then. "Sometimes a person does something so many times in life that they leave an echo after they pass. Their soul isn't here, but the memory of them pouring coffee or walking up the stairs remains embedded in this world for a time."

A cabbage didn't roll across the floor so many times it burned an image into the universe. My grandfather didn't drag bodies around in tarps that many times either. How did that explain my ability to interact with the memories or the porch light dreams?

Either Lorraine was full of shit, or she was way in over her head and was about to find out.

"Well," Robert said, rubbing the back of his neck. "The sooner the better."

"If you're ready to begin, I can call a séance and speak directly with the spirits."

At this point the sound of damp feet running across the tiles came from behind us. The girls emerged from the bathroom with wet, brushed hair and fresh clothes. Amy was standing in the hall listening to the conversation. Her face vacant and unmoving.

"What about the kids?" I asked.

"It would be best if they weren't here," Lorraine said.

"Paul can take the girls out for ice cream," Robert offered.

At that, the teenager let out an annoyed growl. "Why can't you take them? They're your daughters, or did you forget that?"

I tried to shrink in my chair as the two began to argue. From what I'd seen, Robert didn't interact nearly enough with the girls. They always ran to Amy or Paul and only to their father when prompted. Their older brother was the one who moved the girls into the rec room.

Maybe this was just how families operated when there was one sibling much older than the others. A sort of parental figure emerged when the parents were too old or distracted to care for the younger children. It had to be difficult, having three kids.

"I can take them," I offered. The obvious didn't need to be stated. While they were my ghosts, this wasn't my house. I didn't need to be here at all.

That, and I didn't know if I wanted to see how Lorraine freed souls from a nexus event. I imagined her boney fingers plucking dead flies from a spider's web, only those flies were my family. *My dream.*

Both Robert and Paul stopped mid-sentence and stared at me as if they were gauging the idea. It solved the problem, right? Paul would be witness to the excitement and Robert would have the kids somewhere else.

"That's a great idea," Amy said. "The girls really like Mindy."

My heartstrings pulled at that. The truth was that I really liked them too. Even though I didn't want kids, it didn't mean I disliked them. It just wasn't for me. If anything, it was easier to appreciate children when they weren't a full-time job.

"Are you sure?" Robert asked.

"I... don't really want to see this happen," I said. *If it happened at all.*

"Okay," Lorraine said. "It's decided. We'll begin once the girls and Mindy leave."

22

ATTACHMENT

H ands neatly folded in their laps, the girls rode in the Outback like little princesses being charioted to their next event. It was all I could do to contain my grin as I pulled onto the road.

"Mommy said we're getting ice cream?" Charity asked.

"That's right," I confirmed. "I was thinking of that place where you can choose your own toppings."

Lacy's eyes grew large. "Whatever we want?"

"Yup," I said. "Whatever you want."

I wasn't their mom, so it didn't matter to me if they filled up their little cups with candy and ate it by the spoonful. Amy didn't strike me as the type of parent who fussed over every single thing they ate. Besides, given the situation, I wasn't certain anyone's minds were on the nutritional value of ice cream.

Scoops of reckless joy piled high on their ice creams. Lacy wanted the sweet, the sour, and the gummy dumped on her single scoop. Charity was more cautious.

"The flavor doesn't matter," Lacy told her. "What matters are the toppings."

I disagreed. Then again, I wasn't about to put any of that junk on my ice cream. Charity looked up at me and asked, "What flavors are you getting?"

"Lemon and strawberry sherbet. You can get two different flavors if you want."

The five-year-old nodded before settling on one scoop of chocolate and one vanilla. She was so reserved and cautious. It was heartbreaking. The haunting and the stay in the motel had taken its toll on her. Old enough to remember, how could anyone explain it to her when we didn't understand it ourselves?

Holding her cup with both hands, Charity scanned the rows of plastic containers of brightly colored candies. She moved past them despite their calling. Barely able to reach the counter, her eyes went full moon at the maraschino cherries. Bingo!

The three of us sat together without conversation. Each eating our ice cream—or cherries—and enjoying the simplicity of it. No boogey-man, no mediums or nexus events. Just our chosen sweets, probably the first choice they'd made for themselves in a long time.

"Is that lady going to make it go away?" Charity asked.

"We hope so," I said.

"How?" Lacy's tone mirrored my own skepticism.

"I have no idea."

The girls resumed eating their ice cream while they pondered on that. I imagined it was a strange thing for them, grownups not having all the answers. Was it a point of relief or another source of anxiety?

"Mama said you might take us to the mall," Charity said. The shift in conversation was so abrupt. Was that normal? Did kids often veer from paranormal to mall shopping like a flip of a coin? Maybe I should've picked up more babysitting jobs as a teen. I was a little out of my depth.

"Yeah," I said. "I like Bath and Body Works. We can smell all the things in there."

"Is there a toy store?" Lacy asked.

"Maybe," I honestly never noticed. There had to be, right? "We'll check."

I was helping the girls throw their cups in the trash when my vision blacked out. It was only for a moment but jarring enough for me to hesitate. Glancing around the room, I waited for it to happen again. Nothing.

"Mindy?" Lacy asked.

"Coming."

Shaking the incident off as a random blip or the early stages of a migraine, I got the girls into the car and drove across the street to the mall parking lot. It was within walking distance, and I was driving under fifteen so even if my vision did that again, I couldn't do too much damage.

With the slam of the car door, it happened again. An instantaneous blackout for less than a second. The stress of the last few months must've caught up to me. Sudden sounds seemed to be the trigger. Migraine. There was nothing more precise than a period on vacation or a headache at the worst time.

Bath and Body Works was definitely not the place to visit when trying to offset a massive headache. The plan shifted in my mind as we walked under the fluorescent lights that blurred my peripheral vision. The chatter around us began to echo straight to the delicate bones around eyes and sinuses.

Get some toys, get back to the apartment and get some Excedrin. The girls could play with their new loot and watch TV while I coped. Who knew how long it took to banish spirits or a basilar migraine. Might as well prepare for an overnighter.

"Here's a toy store," I said. "I'll tell you what, you can each pick out something, and we can all go back to my place."

Their eyes lit at the prospect of getting toys that neither of them seemed to hear much else. While they ran around the store, I texted Amy to let her know where we were going and my address in case she needed to pick up the kids. Migraines either slam me over the head or just threaten for days at a time. I had no way of knowing which one it was going to be.

"How is it going so far?" I asked.

"She's just sitting on the floor like she's meditating," Amy replied.

Not sure what I expected. It wasn't like Lorraine came in with a ghost vacuum or holy water. Maybe all she had to do was sit there and commune with the spirits? I'd tried that several times and it resulted in nothing but a cabbage sighting.

My vision went black again, only this time it stuck. Something was moving within the darkness, like static. Frozen in place, the porch light flipped on, and I saw Lorraine under the light. She was on her knees, hands outstretched like she was reaching for it.

And then...

I was in the toy store again.

The sudden mobility sent my knees knocking and I had to lean against a Barbie stand. Charity and Lacy were oblivious. For all her uncertainty, Charity was cradling the same doll as she followed her older sister around as she inspected something encased in plastic.

Okay. This wasn't a migraine.

"Did you two find something you like?" I asked.

Charity clutched her doll tight, but Lacy was still trying to case the place for that perfect toy. "Let's hurry up," I said. A cold tingle climbed my spine as I forced a smile. "I have all the good channels. And popcorn."

One of those things prompted Lacy to make her selection. It was a doll that had several outfits and hair that changed colors when it was wet. Just in case, I grabbed a few more random toys at the cash register before ushering the girls out.

Whatever was happening, I didn't want it to happen while I was at the mall or driving two young children around.

The drive home was less than ten minutes, but my knuckles blanched as I clutched the steering wheel. At any moment, the porch light could come on and I'd be behind the wheel. Freaking out about it wasn't going to help either. I was so on edge that I swerved over a paper bag in the road.

Glancing in the rearview mirror, the girls were too involved with their toys to notice.

"What are you going to name them?" I asked.

Charity had already considered this. "Suzy."

"I don't know what to call mine," Lacy's voice had a slight whine to it. "The box says her name is Lucy, but that's too close to my name."

Three stoplights away from home. I could do this. If only I could get my heart to stop pounding like it was going to launch into the intersection. "I'm sure she wouldn't mind if you changed her name to something else."

"I can't think of any good names."

Lacy was either tired or hungry. I recognized the tone and length of her complaints. "Are you hungry?"

"No."

"Oh, well I'm hungry. Maybe we can order a pizza."

Charity gasped. "The kind with the cheese in the crust?"

The only kind of pizza worth having. "Of course."

Lacy remained quiet. She was either pouting or considering the merits of stuffed crust. We passed the last streetlight and my body started to relax as the apartment complex came into view.

Maybe Lorraine was a legit medium doing something about the ghosts. I wasn't certain why that was the conclusion I came to. It could've been just the opposite. She might've been making things worse, increasing the strength of the haunting to a point where it could happen while I was awake.

Another possibility was that these visions were just a kind of anxiety. A physical manifestation of all my fears and internalized stress over the last few months taking a new shape in my mind.

Whatever it was, it happened again.

Instead of cutting straight to black, the porchlight was on, and Lorraine was still under it. Her hands reaching and swaying like she was moving to a rhythm I couldn't hear. Shawl on the ground around her, the light of the porch created a kind of ethereal glow.

I didn't know what this meant. What was happening? When her arms reached higher, they seemingly stretched beyond natural means. Just as her fingertips reached the light, an awful crunch sounded in the dead silence. Her thumb dislocated, then her ring finger.

One by one, the medium's fingers were snapping and twisting in different directions. I couldn't move, I couldn't scream. My body wasn't in this place.

"Mindy!" Lacy screamed.

"What?" I asked. Whirling around, I found myself still in the car with the seatbelt on. My foot was on the break pedal, but we were stopped in the middle of the driveway. A car behind me was so annoyed, he honked and drove around, giving me a mean stare and a middle finger as he passed.

"Are you okay?" Lacy asked.

Charity didn't say anything. She just clutched her doll and tried her best to be a big girl and not cry. My heart was racing and I was trembling like my blood sugar had a sudden drop.

"How long have we been stopped?"

"Just like a minute, but it was like you couldn't hear me," Lacy said.

"I'm sorry, I got distracted. I'm just really worried about what's happening at your house."

Lying to them wouldn't help. It certainly didn't protect me from my lineage or Gail from an investigation. It might be going against what their parents told them, but I wanted them to know I would be honest no matter what.

"Sometimes, I see the ghosts too," I said, trying to steady my voice.

"The boogeyman?" Charity whispered.

"Yeah," I said, parking the car in my reserved spot. "The lady your dad brought over is supposed to help, but she might not be able to."

"Sometimes he yells at night, but I don't think he knows we can hear him," Charity said.

I frowned at that. They never told us that before. "What does he say?"

Charity hesitated and Lacy looked at her sister and nodded. "It's okay, she's not our mom."

Inhaling a big breath, the little girl gave her best impression of an old, frustrated man. "Jesus Christ, Kimberly Agnes!"

There's something violently hilarious about a child cussing. Even more so because the girls had no context. Erupting into giggles, the contagion spread to the girls, and they too began to laugh.

"Kim is my mother—his daughter," I explained. "She was always in trouble as a little girl."

Mom was always in trouble as an adult too.

The sisters' shared the same expression before Lacy said, "He's just a scary dad."

"He also can't hear, so he doesn't realize how loud he is."

Charity's face screwed up. "Mama said that when people go to heaven, all their ouchies go away."

"He's not in heaven yet. He's stuck. That's why we called Lorraine."

But there was a chance Grandpa would be unable to leave the house. He'd be alone and forever cursing my mother just like the rest of us.

"Did something happen?" I texted Amy.

I needed confirmation that my visions were just a migraine brought on by stress and anxiety. Not some psychic link to the farm or a dire warning.

The girls sat on the living room floor with popcorn and their toys strewn about while they argued over which movie they wanted to watch. They agreed on Tinkerbell, but there were three different films. Lacy wanted to watch the pirate one and Charity wanted to watch the one with the magical beast. Either way, they were distracted.

There was no response.

Charity caved and the two were watching Pirate Fairy while I marveled at the separation between our worlds. There I was, fearing that the medium was getting her fingers broken and rearranged while the girls remained oblivious.

That was the goal after all. To shield them from danger and allow them to remain children even if Paul no longer could. But I couldn't help but imagine myself at their age, my grandparents were the ones trying to protect me from danger.

People always claim that there's some larger understanding of life once you have kids of your own, and maybe that was true in some respects, but universally I felt like protecting kids was just a given.

But there's a difference between protecting them and protecting the adult ego.

It's one thing to stop a toddler from riding their tricycle on a freeway, and another to share your feelings. The girls didn't need to know that I saw Lorraine's fingers snapping like candy canes but letting them know I was worried didn't hurt. If anything, it meant they weren't babies for feeling worried either.

Robert was still denying Paul insight despite being an active member of the family, and I felt like that's where most of their conflict came from. The son wanted the truth. It didn't need to be in the form of financial statements, but he was old enough to understand his parents weren't wealthy people.

I didn't need to know my grandpa murdered my father, but knowing he passed away might have helped me process things growing up. At least I wouldn't have spent so much time fantasizing about my father's glorious return. Banishing Mom's stupid boyfriends and making my life better for it.

Sometimes I imagined he'd be in a large, wrapped Christmas present like the toy soldier in The Nutcracker. Other times he was an unexpected knock at the door where we instantly knew one another.

On TV, the young Captain Hook was screaming as he flailed around, trying to fly. The girls were laughing as Tinkerbell saved the awkward soon to be villain.

My phone buzzed.

"Lorraine won't wake up from her trance. I don't know if this is normal or what."

Jolted back into the darkness. I saw Lorraine. Her pose remained unchanged, but all her fingers were badly broken. Wrists buckled and her arms painfully entwined around one another. Just another fixture in the setting, I was unable to move, but maybe I could call her.

"Lorraine? Lorraine, you need to wake up."

I had no idea if I was actually speaking or just yelling in my head. The peacocks were still cawing and the crickets still chirping, but it felt synthetic somehow. Like someone was playing a recording of the noises on the farm the way I remembered it. The way I liked it.

The reality was probably a woman screaming in agony as she twisted like a pretzel on the patio.

"Lorraine, wake up and get out of here."

I didn't get a response, just more cracking as her spine snapped out of place. Why could I hear that and not her voice? Lorraine's head fell back. There was another series of snaps before her bloodshot eyes locked on me. Could she see me?

"Wake up!"

"Find the center," Lorraine's voice came from the fog rolling across the orchard.

Railing against the paralysis in this state, I could feel my muscles tensing against the resistance. An arm got free. I took a swing but hit the back of the couch.

Panting, I stared at the pictures of Christian and I on our wedding day. His nervous smile and my enormous hair under a veil. I was back in my apartment. The girls were watching Captain Hook betray Tinkerbell.

Phone still locked in my hand. Amy's text was two words.

"She's dead."

23

Unclean Break

L orraine was dead.

I had watched it happen, but it didn't feel real. Just like that, a whole life and reality was gone. An entire solar system of people and experiences that once revolved around the woman were left in the dark without warning. Something in my chest hitched and I used my sleeve to wipe my eyes.

The girls were finishing up the movie. I had to get it together before they turned around and saw my face. So much for honesty. But I was not about to tell them that the woman died in their house.

"Dead?" I texted back. I doubted she'd text me back. They were probably calling the police, freaking out, doing whatever it was you did when someone died in front of you. Poor Paul. I wished he'd come with us. He was a man in his own right, but even grown men don't deserve to see such things.

What would this mean for the girls? There's no way they could stay in the house after this. If Lorraine's death happened the way I saw it, there's no way. I wouldn't let them. I'd tell them to come live with us until they could save enough for their own place. I'd burn it to the ground before the girls returned.

"Do the two of you want blankets and pillows?" I asked.

"Yes please," Lacy said as she tried to put on a different movie.

"I want to watch the Neverbeast!" Charity was threatening to tantrum.

"Lacy, you picked first," I said. "Now it's your sister's turn."

The little girl huffed and muttered, "Fine."

Both were fading fast. It wasn't even six yet, but they were getting grumpy. I got some blankets and pillows out of the hallway closet. About that time, the front door opened, and Christian stepped through the door.

"Oh, hey girls!"

My heart dropped at the sound of his voice.

Ready to rush to his arms and sob, I couldn't because I didn't want Charity and Lacy to see and realize something went terribly wrong. It was like holding my breath as I got the girls settled into their makeshift beds on the floor.

Christian pulled me in and gave me a chaste kiss on the cheek. "Hey, honey. How's everything going?"

"Fine," I managed, but he already knew everything wasn't fine. He tensed for a moment but recovered.

"Oh, I need to show you some work stuff," Christian said. "Girls, we'll be right back."

Neither of them noticed, too engrossed by the TV as they nestled into the blankets. He led me to the bedroom and once the door clicked, I let out that breath.

He held me while I told him everything and showed him the texts. Christian was frowning and his chest puffed like he was angry. "Do we know how she died?"

"I saw it."

"You were there?" His voice raised like he was furious, but I think he was just scared.

"No, in my dreams. They started happening while I'm awake. Just flashes, but it was just like the porch light dreams only she was in it."

There was no telling what was going on in Christian's mind. He believed me, that was something I felt on a cellular level, he just didn't know what it meant. I didn't know either.

"She was being broken, twisted up," I said. "I tried to call to her, tell her to wake up, and that's when Amy told me she'd died."

"I won't lose you to this," he promised.

There was nothing I could say, so I responded with my yearning for him. My only dream come true.

#

Little giggles echoed from the kitchen. I opened my eyes and saw that Christian was no longer beside me. Smiling, I rolled over and was greeted by the smell of pancakes. He was making them breakfast.

I came out just as the plates hit the table.

"Morning," he said. "I thought I'd let you sleep. Amy is going to be here soon to get the girls."

Lacy and Charity were totally unbothered, dumping syrup on their plates until it created a pancake soup. My stomach churned at the idea of something so sweet for breakfast. I ate a banana instead.

"She's not going back there with them, is she?"

He shook his head before lowering his eyes. There was something he wasn't telling me. Something he couldn't say in front of the kids. The banana was a mistake. Right away the nausea was compounded with heartburn.

When the knock came to the door, I was the one who answered. Amy came in, red-eyed and weary. Clearly not ready to drive anywhere, I took her outside where we walked around the complex. If there was ever a time for a cigarette, it was now.

I offered her one and she readily took it.

"They think it was an aneurysm," she said, trembling as she lit the cigarette.

We both knew that wasn't what happened. I didn't need to give her the details for her to know exactly how Lorraine died.

"Where's Paul?"

"Waiting in the car. I'm taking the kids back to Colorado. If Robert wants to stay, that's his business. I can't allow the kids to be in that house anymore."

Even after what happened, Robert wanted to stay? The kids were thrown into a pit, the doors blasted from the frame, and now Lorraine. He really was determined to keep the place. It just didn't make sense. I couldn't help but wonder if Robert was somehow drawn to the property the way I was except maybe he wasn't aware of it. Unlike me, he was willing to lose his family. Something wasn't right.

"Just until everything is packed, right?"

"No," she said with a laugh. "He's in full blown denial. I don't know what's wrong with him."

"I'd do the same if I were you," I said.

There was a moment between us then. Not exactly a goodbye, but a silent commiseration. Amy and I may have never gotten along as much as I hoped we would, but she was doing the right thing. She had a strength I appreciated. Knowing when to walk away was one thing, but this woman had the strength to actually do it. I wished more women did.

That was when Christian came out with the girls in tow. "I got to get to work," he said with a tone of apology.

"That's okay, we're in for a long drive."

"Where are we going?" Lacy asked.

With a forced smile, Amy leaned down and said, "We're going to see Oma and Opa."

The girls broke into shrill cries of joy and booked it for the car where Paul waited in the passenger seat. We locked eyes. He nodded and I nodded in return.

You're a good man, Paul.

I wanted to watch them grow up. If he was this cool as a teen, what would he be like as a father? What would Lacy and Charity be like as they got older? If they never came back, I'd have to be satisfied with pictures and updates online. Never part of their lives, just cheering from the void.

"Robert says he's coming to work," Christian said with a frown.

Her cigarette shook between her fingers. "We won't be here when he comes home."

"You have amazing kids," I hugged her then. "You're doing what's best for them."

There might still be time to fix this. They could come back, and we could remain close. The family I didn't have.

"Lorraine told me what needs to be done," I said. "I'm going to try—"

"Mindy, stop. This isn't your fight. You're not responsible for everything your family did. It's Robert's fault for not researching the property before buying it."

She didn't understand. It wasn't out of a sense of guilt or some kind of hero complex. I was haunted no matter where I went. No matter how far I fled, the porch light remained on in my mind. Welcoming me home no matter the time or how long I'd been away.

We said our goodbyes, but resentment lingered and festered. How dare this spirit wreck and take lives? It had turned my entire world upside down and took the Miles family on a horror ride that would leave the girls scared and traumatized for life. Every time I went to the farm to confront it, I'd always done so with the gentle reproach of encountering Grandpa.

I came with love and questions in the attempt to soothe whatever ills left the farm in its current state, but now, I just wanted to yell at it. To light the place on fire and watch it burn.

Okay, so I'm not an arsonist, but I couldn't sit with the powerless anger anymore.

I waited until Christian went to work. Saying nothing about what I had in mind. He probably already knew.

That meant he understood there was no stopping me.

The farm was as it always was. It sat on its hilltop and observed the world around it with the disinterest of a tree in winter. So comfortable in its power. As if it were satisfied that it had once again gotten its way. I marched inside the house, ready to tell it exactly how I felt.

"Are you happy now?" I yelled. "Chased off another perfectly good family. Pushed away people who wanted to love you the way I loved you."

Of course, the house didn't speak back. I wasn't done.

"Answer me," I said. "Or I'm going to walk out and never come back."

It could haunt me with dreams for the rest of my life — or its life — the only thing that kept this place from being bulldozed was the silo. A few good whacks with a mallet would destabilize it. The owls would need to find a new home, but it's not like they could prove anything.

I'd damage it just enough that one windy storm could knock it down and the property would become a developer's playground.

"With the silo gone, Robert might be able to sell this place for profit," I said.

I growled and stomped my foot before turning around to make good on my promise. The only feeling I got within the house was my own anger mirrored back at me. Like it was taunting me. No memories or rattling doors. Just my own bitterness filling up an empty space.

It was like the house was trying to gaslight me.

Whatever. I was going to do some damage.

There's a single step from the porch to the gravel driveway. Only, when I took that step, I missed.

Rough hands grabbed my right hand. Off balance, I assumed it was Christian trying to catch me as my foot fell through the ground like I'd missed several steps, but he wasn't here. I was alone when I shouldn't have been.

The hands pulled my arm behind my back. Muscles strained as I tried to get away, but the arm twisting behind my back was the only thing that kept me from freefalling. The unseen person pulled my arm even further up my back. Bones are not meant for rotation. My arm fractured. Pain coiled and splintered as the shoulder was forced to relinquish its hold.

I screamed, and then, there was nothing.

24

HOUSEBOUND

Persistent and intrusive, just when I thought I had the answer to the question on the test, another beep would sound, and I'd forget again. I didn't know what sort of test it was, and I couldn't recall the question anymore because of that damned beep. I searched for it, but my mind was an empty room. It was so frustrating that I had no choice but to open my eyes.

Beep...Beep...

The noise was coming from a nearby machine. Plastic and a series of tubes and wires came from it. I was sore. Not like after a good workout, more like I was hit by a truck. My whole side throbbed. It was so hot and itchy, I tried to move my arm, but it was heavy. Encased in something.

"She's awake," Gail said to someone. I frowned. Why the hell was Gail here?

"Christian?"

Her soft hand found mine. "It's all going to be okay."

Well, yeah, but–"Where's Christian?"

I was in a hospital bed. The last thing I remember was someone grabbing my arm and twisting it back at the farm. Judging by the cast, they succeeded. "What happened?"

"We were hoping you could tell us," Gail said. "Whatever happened, it's not your fault. And you know you can stay with me."

What the hell was she talking about? It took a few blinks before Gail came into focus. Her skin was red and patchy from crying. Her perfume was so strong it was burning in my sinuses. My throat was dry, and it felt like I had socks on my teeth. I tried to reach for the cup of water on the nightstand but forgot that my arm didn't work.

Gail retrieved the cup and bent the straw to help me get a few sips of water. "I went to the farm," I said. "I tripped and someone grabbed my arm..."

"Did you see who?"

I shook my head. "It all happened so fast."

That's when a doctor came in. A slender Asian man with glasses and a long white coat. "Hey, she's awake."

"I want my husband."

"Of course," he said, but I noticed the way his eyes shifted to Gail who was wiping her eyes with a tissue. "We just have a few questions."

He got a stool and wheeled it over before sitting beside us. "Do you know what a spiral fracture is?"

I'd never broken a bone in my life, so no.

"It's when a bone undergoes so much strain that it splinters without fully snapping. We had to perform surgery. This kind of break is never an accident. We see it in domestic violence incidents."

Oh, no. My heart fell to the floor. They thought Christian had attacked me. I was already shaking my head, trying to deny it. "It wasn't Christian. He was at work."

I turned to Gail and said, "Gail, he'd never hurt me. Not ever. You know he was at work, why would you accuse him?"

My words carried as much weight as a sheet of paper.

At that, I tried to sit up, but the doctor gently pushed me back down. I looked at the location, but the entire thing was casted with pins sticking out of the sling.

"Did you get a look at the assailant?"

"Strong," I said. "It was like he wasn't even trying."

"He had to be trying," the doctor rebutted.

"His hands were huge. His fingers went all the way down to my chest. One on my shoulder and the other on my wrist."

The doctor was nodding like he was hearing something he needed to hear. "That matches the bruise on your shoulder."

"Can you show me?"

Quick to oblige, the doctor wheeled to the other side of the bed and carefully pulled down the hospital gown. "Hand me that mirror, would you?" he asked Gail.

Showing me the mark, I cringed on the inside. A massive, hand-shaped bruise the color of ripening plums wrapped around my shoulder. This was proof enough that Christian didn't do it. The hand was larger than his by far.

"We took pictures already, but the police will want a report."

"Can I see my husband now?"

Gail withered in the corner of the room. If she had her way, he'd be thrown in jail no matter what I said. Why was she so quick to accuse him? I'm not my mom, and Christian wasn't anything like her boyfriends.

"Christian is my Power of Attorney," I said, scowling at Gail. "You needed his consent to perform the surgery. I know he's out there waiting."

"I just want to make sure you're safe," Gail said.

"Look at this hand," I leaned my shoulder toward her and watched her flinch. "Bring Christian in and compare his hand to this, you know he didn't do it."

"That's not a bad idea, actually." The doctor said as he left the room.

"Marv had hands like that," Gail uttered. "He always talked about his Scandinavian roots. How he had Viking blood in his veins."

That's when it occurred to me.

Grandpa's ghost wasn't the malicious spirit haunting the property. It was my father's vengeful spirit. Already a violent man, he was angry for the way he died and wanted to remain on the property to torment anyone who dared call it a home. To scuff what little pride my family had. To ruin the legacy of gentle prosperity by my grandparents.

"He never left," I told her.

Fuming with the notion that my mother's abuser found a way to live on when he was so undeserving. That he dared lay his hands on me. And Gail for accusing Christian despite all logic. Gail stopped sniffing and stared at me with wide eyes. I didn't know what was going on in her mind, and I didn't care.

My eyes found Christian rushing into the room. A blur of beige, still wearing his Carhartt. Dark shadows corroded around his eyes. How long was I out? He hadn't slept since.

His hands reached to embrace me, but he hesitated before a sob broke out. "I don't know how to touch you without hurting you."

"I'm okay," I assured, but he was shaking his head. Too rattled to argue, his eyes focused on the pins that skewered my arm. "I'll be okay."

A surge of dreaminess worked through my veins. Painkillers probably. I wouldn't argue with him right now, but there was no way in hell I was going to run away from this. If Marv could do this to me, just imagine what he could do to Lacy or Charity, or anyone else who tried to move in.

Wanting revenge from the dead is a fruitless venture.

Anger is a part of grief. When we can't be angry at the dead, we lash out at the living. Family members can become casualties surrounding a hospital bed when the machines are turned off. If it's an illness, a person can lash out at the cancer that ate their loved one inside out. The drunk driver or the senseless random violence that occurs when anyone can buy a gun.

When Mom died, my resentments carried on, only she wasn't there to receive it. It was her fault she died. I know addiction is a disease, but it wasn't addiction that killed her. She simply gave up. Dislodged herself from the world and life ceased to happen.

The sheriff said we were lucky the lit cigarette in her mouth didn't fall out and catch fire. That we were smart to get her renter's insurance. We did all the right things because we knew she never did. I was livid at that too.

She should've been present in my life, offering motherly advice and support, not baggage. But issuing demands and complaints was Mom's love language. Nothing was ever good enough for her. It was like she was afraid that if she was content no one would have a reason to talk to her. But that's all I ever wanted. To have someone I could tell everything to without guilt.

I couldn't get that from Mom, but I could get revenge on Dad. Not just for the arm, but for everything else he broke on his way to me.

I was looking at a minimum of four months in a cast. Possibly six depending on how things healed.

Pictures were taken of the bruise on my shoulder. While Christian wasn't written off the suspect list entirely, the detectives were certain it wasn't him. Between the watertight alibi and the bruise, his name was just a formality at best.

"It's not just the size of the hand," the man on the phone said. "It's the overall torque required. We're looking at a man closer to six foot five. Your husband isn't a large man by any means. He'd struggle to do this kind of damage."

When it was time to leave the hospital, I noted that Gail and Christian had some sort of agreement. I sat in a wheelchair, doped up to oblivion trying to decipher just what it was they were up to.

"Gail going home?" I asked as he helped me into the car.

"I asked her to stop by," he said. "Keep an eye on you while I'm working."

I was shaking my head, but it felt slow and wasn't getting the message across. "I'll be fine."

"I'd feel a lot better if someone was with you," he said. "Besides, I think she's still convinced I did it."

I didn't need a babysitter. I had enough painkillers to last me a lifetime. All I needed was a cozy spot on the couch and the remote. Not Gail fussing over me.

This would complicate things. I didn't have any ideas on how to uproot my dad's spirit, but acquiring ideas would be even harder with Gail watching my every move. Being helped into the car, Christian fastened my seatbelt for me in the way I used to fasten the seatbelt for Grandma and Mom as their health declined.

It wasn't forever, but maybe I did need help. If it made Christian feel better and allowed him to focus on his work, then I'd cooperate. Gail would see that my husband was not a wife-beater. After a week of dedicated rest, my aunt would be satisfied that she did all she could, and Christian would stop making those worried glances like I was about to shatter into a thousand pieces the moment he wasn't looking.

#

For the first week, I did need help. I hated it when Gail was right. At least she was wrong about Christian. I'd need to hang on to that one for the rest of her life, but when it came to functioning with a broken arm, she was right.

It was all the little things. Using the bathroom. Opening bottles of antibiotics. Plugging my phone into a charger. My pillow fell off the bed and guess who couldn't reach down to get it? Basic functions I took for granted had become uphill battles that I didn't anticipate until I went to move my left arm and was reminded with a soul-wracking ache.

Between the pain that precisely came an hour before the next dose of painkillers and the sleep that came thirty minutes after Gail came in with the drugs, my life was a revolving schedule of pain, eat, drink, pill, and once again sleep.

Showering was exhausting. It took so much effort that I'd collapse in bed afterwards, sleep the rest of the day, and find myself awake at night. Something about the drugs spurred my need for a smoke too. Being high was like drinking, my inhibitions were short circuited and I needed pleasure in any way possible.

"Gail..." I groaned. "Gail..."

"What?" she asked, stepping into the room.

Asking my aunt for a cigarette felt weird. Like asking the high school teacher to buy a round of shots. "Can you do me a huge favor?"

She stood there clicking her tongue like she was annoyed. "I'm here, aren't I?"

"I really want a smoke."

Gail shook her head and left the room. Laying in bed, I wondered if she was going to get me a cigarette or just let me suffer, but a few minutes later I heard the front door shut. Closing my eyes, I whispered, "Yes!"

I don't know if it was the relief of knowing she was going to buy me a pack or what, but I fell back asleep immediately. My mind was still worrying that she'd buy the wrong brand — I only liked the one — but given the circumstances, I'd be happy with whatever she got.

Those were the thoughts I had while I stood pain free in the driveway of the farm, staring at the porch light. Even in a drug induced stupor, my mind was transported to the farm where I stared at the same place regardless of the day or time. It was currently raining.

"Can't I get a break?" I asked no one. "Even for a nap?"

Rain fell like a shower, tinging along the metal roofs of the sheds. At least I didn't feel wet or cold. I was just another fixture on the property.

My leg was jiggling. I looked down but they weren't moving.

"Wake up," Gail said. "I got your damn cigarettes."

Opening my eyes, I was back in bed, and she was dangling a pack of Winstons over me. I gasped and reached for them, but my aunt jerked away. "If you're going to smoke, at least do it outside."

I scowled at her. Of course I'd smoke outside. I wasn't my mom.

She helped me outside and bundled me in a blanket while I lit up. "Thanks," I said. "I rarely smoke but sometimes I just need one."

"I figured it was the drugs talking. Your mom smoked like a chimney."

"You know, I've never actually seen her finish a cigarette."

Gail released a dry cackle at that. "Come to think of it, neither have I."

Mom had this terrible habit of lighting a cigarette, taking a few drags only to leave it in the ashtray and forget about it. New room? New cigarette. It was like she thought they were incense and wanted to keep them lit all about the house. It was disgusting.

"I'm so glad you got Winstons, they're the only kind I smoke."

Gail's face was somewhere between laughter and concern. "That's really funny."

"Why?"

"I only got them out of habit. Dad smoked Winstons my entire life. He quit a few years before you were born."

Something about that set my stomach churning. The smell of the cigarette reminded me of the half-smoked pack I found in my pocket.

"Did he smoke half of them and put them back in the soft case?"

Grunting in disgust, Gail confirmed the fear. "Yes, it stunk so bad Mom had to tell him to knock it off."

I put the cigarette out and dropped it into the empty coffee tin we kept for such occasions. "I think I'm good now."

Christian came in every night weary and fretting. At some point we switched sides on the bed so he could cuddle against me on my good side. More than once I wanted to give him one of my pain meds just to help him get some sleep. He'd always refuse, unable to help the fact that he was a naturally straight-laced man. Even in his rebellious era, Christian couldn't hang. He ate a pot brownie once and thought he was going to die, so maybe it was better this way.

"I'm feeling better and stronger every day," I assured him as he drifted off to sleep. "It's only a matter of time before I'm on the loose once more."

This was what I said every night. I did it because it seemed to be the only thing that made him smile these days.

"Just don't go where I can't," he'd mutter.

His nightly reminder that he needed me too. It ached in a good way.

Come morning, he'd be off to work again, leaving me to Gail's whims.

For whatever reason, she liked to open the blinds every morning. I didn't ask her to. I'd squint against the sting of the bright morning light. Jolted by pain and brightness. It was like she was trying to aggravate me into getting out of bed to close the blinds before hobbling back to bed.

"Why do you do that?" I asked one morning. The pain in my arm was steadily decreasing and so was the need for pain meds. It took me all week, but I managed to wake before she started her mourning routine.

"So you'll know what the weather is like outside," she said.

"There's no point," I said. "I already know."

Her face puckered and she put her hands on her hips. "Okay, what is it like outside?"

"It's snowing."

I knew this because it was snowing at the farm where I kept watch while I slept. "Not enough to stick."

Without another word, Gail opened the blinds and confirmed it. "You barely leave the bed, how...?"

Christian would've understood, but he'd been working not only his job but my own. I think the work helped him deal with what I was going through. He hated that I was in pain but there was nothing he could do besides make sure the rent was paid and the business didn't fall apart.

In going to the farm alone and trying to fix it myself, I failed him. I went where he couldn't. It was a mistake I wish I could take back. Meanwhile Gail only stared at me like I was about to levitate off the bed.

"Sit down, Gail. I need to tell you what's going on."

Maybe in me telling her my truth, she'd finally tell me hers. It didn't take a genius to figure out that she was more involved with what happened to Marv than she let on. The heartbreak and pain in her eyes at the hospital and the fact that she was still considered a suspect in his death.

There was something she was willing to take to her grave, but that's what got us into this mess in the first place.

I told her about the farm. When I got to the haunted bits, she scoffed and tried to get up. "When you fell out of the yellow Plymouth, you were wearing a pink taffeta dress."

"Grandma told you that."

"It was strapless, and you had a matching shawl. Your hair was long and straight. You were wearing pink lipstick. And long white gloves."

"She could've told you that too."

"You were crying," I insisted. "You needed to go to the hospital, but your parents couldn't afford to take you. The whole right side of your face was scraped. When you were alone in the bathroom, you slapped yourself in the face over and over until you stopped crying and vowed to never be a poor farm girl again. I think you fell out of the car on purpose."

At that, she sat down.

"The house is haunted. It's haunted by memories, by spirits, and one of those spirits is Marv."

Pressing her lips together, Gail nodded. "I'll never forget that night. He tried to take Kim. When she didn't go quickly enough, he grabbed her arm and she fell—"

"Off the porch step," I finished. "Because that's where it happened to me. These secrets, they find a way to come back and haunt us."

"How did Marvin die, Gail?"

She was shaking her head and sniffing back the tears. "I can't..."

I didn't pity her. Her tears meant nothing at that moment. All of this was happening to me because my family was so determined to keep this from me. All of them knew but me. I'd meandered these broken trails too far in the woods to go back.

"If you don't tell me, the house will."

"Christian won't—"

"Won't let me?" I finished. "Honey, this isn't the sixties anymore. He can't stop me from going back and finishing this."

It was a feeble attempt to dissuade me. She'd probably run to Christian and make him promise her. He'd give her whatever assurances he had to, but we both knew this wasn't going to stop until I undid the nexus event.

Lorraine told me to find the center. I assumed that meant the event itself, but now I wasn't so sure. The house reacted violently when I threatened the silo. It was in the center of the property. Abandoned and loathed, the last reminder that the whole area once belonged to impoverished farmers. Their property values would increase if their neighbor could just tear it down.

That was the center. The nexus event may not have taken place there, but that was where I'd find the spirit holding me hostage.

25

‒ • ‒

THE CENTER

H ealing is tedious work.

Three weeks after the attack, the ache was gone but the top layer of my skin was growing itchy from lack of exfoliation. With the pain medicine reduced to over-the-counter pills, I was able to return to the office. At this point, I'd learned how to maneuver and function with one arm for the most part, but it was still annoying.

After our conversation, Gail went to the detectives and finally told them whatever it was she wouldn't tell me. It was enough to send her home to California but not enough to make her brave enough to tell me as much.

"She didn't even say goodbye," Christian complained when he read the text off my phone.

After the attack, he thought he had to win Gail over in some way. "She knew you had nothing to do with my arm."

"Didn't feel that way at the hospital."

I'd assumed the role of Kim, the youngest daughter as she should've been in my grandparents' eyes, but that wasn't the case for Gail. I was forever her baby sister's daughter. One of Kim's many mistakes. Beholden to keep in touch for the sake of family.

It was easier for her that way, but I think the more she got to know me, the more she began to see what my grandparents saw. Besides, it's hard to admit when someone isn't the fuck up you always assumed they'd be.

"I think it's time to go back," I said.

This conversation went circular in the way arguments often did, only this wasn't an argument so much as a butting of two truths that neither of us could deny.

"It's too dangerous," he'd say.

"I know it is, but what happens when it kills again?" I'd retort.

We were both right, but for Christian, there was culpability in this. I couldn't drive, so it meant he'd have to take me. By taking me to the place that broke my arm, if I got hurt again or worse, it would be his fault somehow. If the roles were reversed, I'd be saying the exact same things.

"I'll take a Lyft if I have to."

I only issued that threat once and immediately regretted it. He didn't respond. Instead, his eyes met mine and while he didn't say the words, they echoed in my mind. *Don't go where I can't...*

Today, the argument would continue. I spent most of the day rehearsing new ways of saying what had already been said, but when I presented my case to Christian, his response left me slack jawed.

"I hate to say it, but you're right," Christian agreed.

The break in the circle caught me off guard.

"I'm right?"

What happened to change his mind? I hurried to sit beside him as he tried to voice a worry he'd been denying for some time.

"It's Robert. He didn't come to work today. I tried calling him but there was no answer."

I knew he was still working for us, but I assumed it was to help pay for the move. Amy said he was in denial, but that was almost a month ago. He should've been close to moving everything out by now.

"Maybe he's finally packed up," I offered.

Christian shook his head. "No. When I asked him about it, he said Amy was just visiting and was coming home soon. That was two weeks ago."

I frowned at that. "Amy made it clear she's not coming back. She told him."

Tossing his hands in the air, he shrugged. "I know, but he is either in denial or... I don't know."

Or a certain farm and its ghosts have found a new person to drag into its clutches. I should've known. The gravitational pull it had on me was so intense it took three weeks and a broken arm to finally realize that I didn't want this.

What my husband wanted to say was that Robert was just as dazzled by the property as I was. He'd never utter that part out loud in fear that it would start a fight. We had too many of those recently. The underlying fear was that if I went back, I'd find myself longing for more. Sometimes I was afraid of that too.

"I'm worried the farm has its claws in him. The way it had me."

Christian froze, the hoodie ill-positioned over his chin. "He never stops talking about it. About his plans and dreams for it. Kinda like you did for a while before it..."

"Tried to drown me? Break my arm? Yeah. We need to go check on him."

The lights were on as we headed up the hill and pulled into the driveway. Except for the porch light. That shouldn't have meant anything to me, but it was the star of my dreams for the last several months so to see it off made me feel strange somehow. Like we weren't welcome.

We never did give back the extra set of keys, but Christian knocked anyway. Neither of us wanted to catch the man unaware.

When he didn't answer, Christian tried the door to find it unlocked and peeked inside.

"Robert?"

The answer was the biting cold wind channeling towards us from the hallway.

"It's freezing in here," he said as we stepped in.

He wasn't exaggerating. The cold leached up from the tiled floors. It was winter, but unless Robert couldn't pay the heating bill, there was no reason for it to be this cold.

"Robert?" I called.

Christian was on high alert, staying a few steps ahead of me, he scanned the room like he was anticipating the worst. Gulping the cold air, I followed the stream of cold that was coming from the hallway.

A memory came to me then. The one that usually brought about laughter and lament at an expensive repair bill. Shattering glass where the moral of the story was that boys do stupid things. This time it wasn't a boy or a single pane.

A shrill panic urged me to the mud room. "Robert!"

My shoes slid on glass, and I almost fell when Christian's arm looped around my waist. We both stopped and stared at the scene.

Robert lay face down on the back patio. Puddles of blood were freezing in the snow. Broken, crimson tinted glass was scattered everywhere. Much like how I reenacted Gail's Dairy Queen accident, Robert had acted out Steven's collision with the sliding glass door.

"Is he dead?" I asked.

Christian moved forward, stepping over the aluminum frame and kneeled beside Robert's prone body. He gave me a terrified glance before rolling Robert over.

I held my breath as Christian checked for a pulse. There was glass and blood everywhere, but his neck was mostly clean. There was a thick shard of it stuck in his forehead where the blood still oozed.

"He's alive," Christian said. "We need to get him warm, call an ambulance."

Stepping backward, I turned and rushed to the bedroom. I didn't know where Amy kept anything, so I tore the comforter off the bed and ran back to Christian.

"Here," I said, tossing it through the door.

He was already on the phone with an ambulance. I wondered if they were tired of coming to the house yet. There was nothing else we could do but the nervous energy was eating at me. I searched the rec room in hopes of something that could help. All the kids' stuff was just where they left it. Their beds were unmade, and their toys were scattered.

No signs of boxes or moving. There were tools scattered about and duct tape like Robert was fixing things around the house. Amy and the kids were gone, but he was content to putter around the house like they were just on a trip to the grocery store. An ick crept over me then. Was this what I would've become had I become the owner?

I shook off that thought. Warmth. Robert needed to get warm. The wood stove would be nice to use, but moving Robert might do more harm than good.

"Keep trying to wake him," I said.

Christian shook him gently and spoke to him. "Hey, buddy, you're late for work."

Pacing back and forth, it was all I could do to bear the waiting. I grabbed the broom propped up in the corner and swept the way clear. The last thing we needed was a paramedic to slip on the chunks of glass while hauling Robert out. They probably would just walk around the house, but I had to do *something*.

Amy would need to know as well.

That could wait. I'd rather call her to say he's in the hospital and recovering than give her the scenario without answers. Talking to her would only upset the situation. It would have to wait. I hated waiting.

We saw the red and blue flashing lights from the patio.

What felt like hours had only been fifteen minutes. I ran out the front door and waved as the vehicle bobbed along the gravel.

"You're the one who called?" The man in the uniform asked.

"My husband did. We came to check on him when he didn't come to work and found him like this."

Few questions were asked after that. They put him on the stretcher and decided wheeling him through the house would be best. I was sort of relieved my nervous sweeping did amount to something. Based on what little I overheard, Robert was developing hypothermia and had serious blood loss.

I gave them Amy's contact information. "She's visiting family in Colorado."

"He's lucky you guys stopped by. A few more hours and I don't think he would've made it."

Wrapping my arms around myself, I shivered. The farm had already claimed a life this month, it nearly got two. Lorraine managed to escape the nexus. I could sense it the way a cat sensed an impending storm. Her presence was a grounded, confident understanding of the paranormal that would've been noticed among the silent confusion of all the things currently at work on the property. Robert wouldn't have been so lucky.

His spirit would've tangled within the webs and strengthened the haunting that much more.

We huddled together for warmth and watched as the lights flashed against the shadows forming in the overgrown trees and bushes before they faded away. "He'll be okay," Christian said.

He would be. As would the rest of his family or anyone else who lived here. I'd make sure of it.

"I need you to stay here while I do this," I said.

"No. Absolutely not."

The sigh was loud and intentional. I knew he was going to do this, but was I willing to let him come along and see the darkest aspects of my family? It was like giving him a glimpse into every bad thing my family wanted to keep from me. Everything I was. So far the people I loved and wanted to protect had only shown him their worst.

"I don't want you to see them and think they were always like this—they weren't."

"I won't stand here and let something like this happen again," he motioned to my arm. "I know they were good people. I'm capable of understanding that good people do bad things."

But what if he saw something he couldn't unsee? Something that changed us forever?

I cringed through the idea of pushing him away. It would be easier, but it would also be a secret that sat between us on the sofa while we ate sandwiches and watched campy love stories wishing we'd beaten the odds. It was the difference between knowing and hoping that we were going to last.

"Flip on the porch light then," I said.

Christian looked at me then. "Was that it? That was the reason it didn't work last time?"

I shrugged. Not really, it had to do more with my mindset, I think. There was a connection to be sure, but I was approaching this not for answers or demands. I was here to end it. To let go of whatever my grandparents kept from me.

Christian reached inside and flipped the switch. The light broke through the dimness as a young woman pushed right through me. It was Mom. Her red curls braided back and she was wearing an oversized flannel shirt.

A second figure materialized from me then. Towering over her, Marv had long blond hair and a black jacket of some kind. He had one hand on her shoulder and another on the arm twisted behind her back. "Get in the car," he said.

"Get the fuck away from her!"

I turned to see Christian staring slack jawed at a young Gail with long, flat hair. She jumped on the back of Marv, trying to slow him down. Grandpa was bellowing curses from inside the house.

Reaching out, I tried to touch them, but it was only smoke in a mirror. A memory so strong it stained the property red. So, I stepped aside. Committed to watch my father snap my mother's arm like a wishbone with no more wishes. My arm ached as if it were reliving the pain all over again.

Marv reared back and knocked Gail to the concrete. She winced and gasped for air as Mom turned around and pushed Marv back. "You said you'd leave them alone!"

"She was trying to protect them," Christian said.

I didn't take my eyes off the fight in front of me, but he was right. My grandparents were older, Grandpa was still recovering from back surgery. Mom must've agreed to move in with Marv to keep him away from them. My heart hurt as I watched the petite woman flinch and lower to him. It was an act of subservience.

"Come on," she said. "Let's get in the car and go home."

She was so courageous.

Staring down a behemoth, using whatever charms she had to sway him from hurting her family. When they went home, he'd beat her and she knew it, but continued luring him to the car and away from her family.

That was the hardest choice.

Christian slowly wrapped an arm around my shoulders and kissed the side of my head. I didn't realize I was crying until the tears grew hot on my neck. I needed to release these spirits from this event, but Lorraine never told me how.

A blur shot out the door. There was a flash of something silver and a thick crunch. It all happened so fast I fell back on my heels as Christian pulled me close. A wet slap hit the pavement and Mom began to scream.

It was Grandma.

She was barely over five feet, but her arms and shoulders were thick from hard labor. Her brown hair was short and curled around her round face. She came at him in a full sprint and swung sidelong, chopping at Marv's neck with a meat cleaver. His head was still attached but the spine was severed.

He staggered and his head lagged in a sickening way. Like he was nodding off but nodded too hard and his nose hit his chest. His arms swung forward, then back before the rest of his body went with it. Legs ridged, the six-foot-five Marv fell on his back, landing on the cleaver, finishing the job.

My stomach spasmed. I had just enough time to lean over before puking.

Christian let go. He said something like "Nope," before turning around to puke as well.

Mom was screaming as Gail shrank back against the wall of the house. A spray of blood covered her face and Grandpa staggered in the doorway like he was about to faint. It might've been the most horrific moment I'd witnessed in my entire life, but all I could do was stare at Grandma.

How many times did I wish I could see her? Call her on the phone just to hear her voice and forget whatever was bothering me. Listen to her voicemails even when I knew what she was going to say. *"Hello, just me. I wanted to let you know...love you."*

She always told us she loved us. Always. The daughter of a teenage girl who didn't want to have a baby. The first time my great grand-mother told Marjorie Mounts that she loved her was as she lay dying. Grandma wouldn't repeat that history.

And there she was. Right in front of me.

"Grandma?"

She turned in my direction but looked right through me. To them, I was the ghost. I didn't know how much longer I'd have with her. I had moments or a lifetime, so whatever I said to her it had to be good.

"I love you so much."

She was rightfully confused and shaking so hard her knees gave out. Clapping a hand over her mouth, she slumped against the railing. But not before rearing her head back at Mom. Not her face, but her stomach. A sob ripped through me then and I staggered away as the scene blipped out of existence for the last time.

26

— · —

SNOW

I don't know if it's a real memory or not, but it's the earliest one I have. Four or five years old, I have this image in my mind of walking around the driveway while it snowed. The hat was scratchy over my ears, and someone was holding my hand as they led me around. It was like I was living inside a snow globe that had been given a good hard shake for the first time in years.

On the hilltop, we were the first to get snow but it never seemed to last. While it clung like loose cotton on the grassy lands downhill, it was like the gravel leached the moisture, making it hard for the snow to stick. In that memory, the gravel was exposed despite the intense snowfall, so maybe it was real.

Or perhaps it was real simply because I made it real.

Whatever the case, it was snowing when Christian and I stepped off the porch. The air around us was welcome after the agitation-induced heat coursing through our bodies. Neither of us were prepared for the violence the memories reenacted.

"It was Grandma," Christian said.

That explained a lot. Why Gail wouldn't tell me what happened to Marv and her reluctance to tell the police. She was protecting the memory of her mother. The best woman any of us ever knew and never deserved. Gail refused to taint her mother's image even in death. She had no way of knowing how I'd respond to such a thing. *Thank you, Gail.*

"Gail would've rather gone to jail than tell the police the truth."

Christian was still stuck on the images, not the repercussions. "Why the hell did she have a cleaver like that?"

Grandma's meat cleaver wasn't something you could pick up at Wal-Mart. It was a long-handled, thick wedge of stainless steel built for professional butchering. Even then, I don't think it ever occurred to her to use it on a person until she had no other option.

"The slaughterhouse gave it to her," I explained. "When they sent a cow to slaughter, they'd get it back in parts. She needed something to piece it out."

"Jesus."

Everything made a lot more sense now. The decapitation was mostly an accident. Grandpa must've finished the job and removed the teeth so no dental record could be used. Why they went to all the effort of hiding the head in the house I'd never know. Probably a panic-driven reaction to shield Grandma.

"She was protecting her child," I said.

"Well, yeah," Christian said. "When she came at him, you could tell she didn't quite know what she'd do but...damn. Grandma was the sweetest woman in the world. Who knew she had it in her."

You find room when your child is in danger.

We pushed forward toward the silo when something moved. To the left, my old dog Molly sat by the tree. She was covered with oozing scabs and her nails painfully overgrown. I hesitated, not understanding why she was there at first.

I approached her and kneeled to pet her. Her big brown eyes stared at me as her naked tail whacked against the ground.

"What is this?" Christian asked.

"It's Molly, but she never lived here."

How did she get here? She wasn't a memory on the farm. I tried to pet her anyway. Ignoring how my hands shifted through the illusion like she was nothing more than a shallow pool of water. "I'm not sure why you're here, but I love you anyways. I wish there was more we could've done for you."

"Retrievers are known for skin conditions," Christian explained. "Maybe your mom brought her up here?"

"Grandma sold the farm years before we got Molly."

The dog nosed my hand for more pets, but she was already fading. Molly didn't blame anyone for her condition, especially not me. She was a good dog all the way to the end.

I stood only when she was completely gone and tensed as the air shifted. It broke like a fever, and the light from the porch dimmed. Christian must have noticed because he spun around seeking the source.

"Something is changing," he said. "It doesn't feel so heavy."

Lorraine was right.

With each memory we visited and accepted, they were freed from the nexus event. The power that held them here was getting weaker. But that could also mean the event itself might grow desperate and lash out. "We need to be careful."

"Where to next?" he asked.

"Towards the center," I said. Moving against the wind, the snow pelted my face and prickled hot against my skin. We weren't dressed for snow, but I had the feeling it wasn't really snowing. Washington rarely gets snow in December. Looking out at the rest of the landscape, it was hard to tell, but the snow only seemed to be falling on the property.

The porch light flickered and waned like the power was threatening to give out. Good.

Moving toward the milking shed, I could hear the scraping of plastic on gravel. Christian moved to get in front of me but froze when he saw something moving in the darkness. A thick trail parted the gravel, reflective and blue. I patted Christian on the back and stepped out from behind him.

"It's just Grandpa."

It was strange to me now. How could I ever assume he killed anyone? Hunched and staggering, his stiff ankles refused to budge in his slippers. He insisted on disposing of the body knowing it made him complicit because he'd be damned if he ever let his wife take the fault.

I assumed he'd done it because that's what he wanted people to think. His lie echoed beyond the grave because he so badly wished it to be true.

When I saw this memory the first time, it wasn't me he was talking to, it was Mom. We sound the same, Gail and Steven confirmed it. He must have heard my voice and thought it was hers.

"Yeah, Mom..." was what he said.

A simple statement with so many emotions behind it. Grandma killed Marv. They needed to help her. I imagined while he carried the body to the manure pits, Grandma must've been in the house dealing with all sorts of emotions. Perhaps the strain of this event was what brought on her Bell's palsy.

What could I say to him? It was so easy with Grandma and Molly. He was the one I felt the most pressure to release because he didn't deserve to be stuck here reenacting this horrible scene for all of time. The ache of my arm needled its way to my chest before exploding with pain. I gasped and I couldn't breathe.

"Mindy?" Christian was holding me. "Mindy, what's wrong?"

It felt like how I imagined a heart attack would feel. The pain was enough to blackout my vision. My heart struggled in my chest, begging for release. My knees buckled and I had the vague understanding that Christian was guiding me downward.

"It's not my fault you died," I said. "It was clogged arteries and old age. It was just your time."

The breath I took was a forced, wheezing one that echoed throughout the farm. Red blood cells bursting through decades of cholesterol plaque from red meat, butter, and dairy. Everyone in my family had high cholesterol. Even mine was veering upward as I got older.

My eyes snapped open. Still in Christian's arms, I watched Grandpa walk away, dragging the tarp with Marv behind him.

"Mom loves you, we both do," Grandpa repeated.

I savored his voice. This would be the last time I'd ever hear it as I watched him fade into the night.

"Is it done?" Christian stuttered. "Are you okay?"

Pressing into his chest, I nodded. "It's okay now. He was just trying to show me what I needed to say to let him go."

Christian looked in the direction of the memory then back at me. "But it had nothing to do with moving the body."

It didn't. *I'm sorry, Christian.*

He either didn't want to or couldn't show me his death. Instead, he chose a memory he wished everyone would remember. He wanted to be the bad guy so that no one would ever blame his wife. "He wanted everyone to believe it was him so badly. I think he wished he was the one to kill Marv so Grandma wouldn't have to live with the guilt."

Christian's furrowed brows suggested he didn't buy it. "I know this is your family and the farm is haunted, but it's just not adding up…"

I was about to ask him why when the porchlight dimmed to a low, yellow light. "Well, whatever the case, it's working."

He wanted to argue about something. I could tell by the way his jaw tensed as his tongue sought the words like they could be found somewhere along his teeth. You won't find logic here, love. "All we can do is keep moving forward," I told him.

Our eyes went upward to the silo behind the cow run and the snow melted mid-air, turning to fat globs of rain.

27

SILO

"It's a lot bigger than I imagined for some reason," Christian said, staring up at the behemoth tin shell. Thick steel beams held it up from the inside, but the panes were a patchwork of rusted sheets threatening to fall.

He was right. The only time I came here was when Mom brought me. We were probably trespassing, but Mom could sweet talk her way out of most things. She and I walked through the property where she gave me all her stories, but she never did acknowledge the consequences.

"Dad paid a boy to go into the shed and shoot the pigeons," she told me. "I caught him with two wounded birds and took them from him. Nursed them back to health."

What she didn't mention — or didn't know — was that pigeon poop is toxic. Grandpa had paid the boy to scare them off so that their droppings didn't land on the cows, making them sick. Mom took those birds and stashed them in the second story of the chicken coop. What happened next was only natural.

The two wounded birds, unable to fly, made a nest and laid eggs. By the time my grandparents got wind of what she'd done, it was too late. She did nurse them back to health, but soon they and their hatchlings had covered the chickens and their feed in poop. The chickens got sick, and they had to put down at least half of them. In saving two birds, she'd killed half a dozen.

Despite the insistence that owls nested in the silo, Christian and I walked into an eerily quiet space. Along the rafters there were tufts of hay and feathers, but no birds. Owls were nocturnal, so maybe they all left to find food, but it smelled cold and lifeless.

"It seems the owls moved on a long time ago," I said.

Christian kicked at the ground, aiming his light downward. "No fresh droppings on the ground. No pellets either."

I don't know why it was upsetting, but it was. The silo served as a reminder that this place was a true farm. The only thing that kept it and the property from being leveled was the endangered owls and now there was no excuse. No reason to remain.

This could be good news for Robert and his family. Once it was confirmed that the owls moved on, the value and interest in the property would triple. They could sell it and move on. Maybe I could move on once something else sat on the hilltop.

The truth was, I didn't want it to change.

Even after everything we'd all been through, I wanted this place to remain just as it did in my memories. That just couldn't be. It was time for me to let go.

"Mindy," Christian's voice cut through the grief. "Something's been bothering me."

He was still struggling to find the right words, but they came out wrong and fraught. "Molly didn't live here, that was your memory. Your Grandpa... It was his death that you had to acknowledge to let him go. I think—"

His thoughts intersected by my own, I knew what he was getting at. Deep down, I knew all along but was too much of a coward to face it.

As if interceding on my behalf, a small child with pale blond hair appeared. No older than Charity, she was bundled in a sweater and windbreaker. Her knitted hat pressed the blunt cut bangs in a sharp line across her forehead. She stared at us with wide blue eyes.

"It's you," he said.

I closed my eyes and let the guilt pour out.

In the center of everything there was one person who couldn't let go. Only she wasn't a ghost, she was alive and forcing all around her to remain the same. Locking her family and friends into this repeating nightmare all because she knew they were keeping something important from her.

A sob broke from my throat. What kind of person would do such a thing? I had always tried to be polite, unintrusive, considerate. I wanted to be good, but there was just something inside of me that needed to lash out.

They lied to me, and I couldn't swallow that anger even though I loved them and understood their reasoning. Somewhere down the line, I became irrevocably angry when they kept me at arm's length. I never needed to know who my father really was, I just needed them to trust me with the truth.

I always knew what he was. No one had to tell me. Somewhere between the muted responses and jerked conversations. The frowning expressions when I wasn't my mother's daughter. The concerning frowns from my mother's old friends we'd happen across from time to time.

"His?"

She would nod, and the conversation would briskly change. Instances and moments compiled in my mind like the profile of the missing person found in the manure pit. I knew and yet they still carried on with the charade. Only in death were they able to reveal the truth and I still hated them for that.

My anger and my need took on a life of its own. My wrought and need for nostalgia reduced this once beautiful place into a rusted trash heap, not even suitable for wild birds. What had I done to myself? To Lorraine and the girls? How could I ever look those girls in the eyes again?

Falling to my knees before my ghost, the words tumbled out. "What have I done?"

Christian was crying. He couldn't even look at me. This was why I didn't want him to come. There was only ever one person haunting this place. I didn't want him to see the real me.

Well, here I was.

If I couldn't have this place, no one could. I was the boogeyman that frightened the girls at night. The beast who huffed and puffed, blowing all the doors down. Blood showers, breaking myself apart and drowning in my own deep-seated rage and yearning. This was me. Who I truly was. No one was safe, not even the two little girls who did nothing wrong.

"I'm a monster. I'm sorry. I'm so sorry."

Even Christian was by design.

I married a builder who put me on the highest shelf. A man who'd bend his body backward to build the things I couldn't. He picked up where my Grandpa left off with the opinion that I did no wrong. One way or another, I'd find myself on this hilltop, climbing over the bodies and fleeing investors. Luring the handsome builder along to rebuild my heart and make it whole again.

In an act of mercy or understanding, the shadow of my childhood stretched out her gloved hand and I took it. Unlike the others, this one was tangible. From the grip to the synthetic fiber rubbing against my bare hands. She was real and this was her home.

"You can stay here if you want," she said.

Maybe that was for the best. If I remained here among the memories and the truth I was denied, I wouldn't have to face the fact that my anger had power. It had consequences. The idea of facing the Miles family or Gail and admitting the truth–wouldn't that just hurt them more?

Did I even deserve their feelings of betrayal or retribution? I'd caused so much pain. Christian could start again. Women would get in line just to watch him work. He didn't need me. If I was capable of haunting an entire property, what else could I do? What if he made me angry? Would I terrorize him as well?

"No, she can't," Christian said.

The firmness in his voice pulled me away from the thoughts of fading into the night with the rest of my nightmarish creations. How could he still be here after everything?

Christian was on me then. Wrapped around me tight, urging me to release the hand I held. "You said I'm your home. You can't leave your home."

I lashed out at him like I did everyone else. "How can you still want me? After everything."

"It doesn't matter," he said, nestling his face into my neck. "None of this matters. I'll build you a home that is all for you. We can create new memories and you can haunt me with all our joy. Just stay with me, please."

I closed my eyes and basked in his promises, knowing full well he'd make good on them. There was no stopping me from just letting go like he said. We could just let the Miles family pick up the pieces and let Gail move on with her life the way she always wanted to. When I called her, it wouldn't be about the past, only the future.

"You've seen what I can do. What if you're next?"

"This isn't you," he whispered in my ear. "I know you. Don't let it trap you again."

He said he knew me. Christian had stared down my absolute worst and was still pulling me back from the brink. The boy with the religious namesake didn't put his faith in God. He put his faith in me.

"I didn't mean to do this," I stammered. "I didn't know this was real..."

We took another step backward towards the door. He wasn't pulling me, more like guiding. Asking — no, begging – me to let go. "You couldn't have known," Christian assured.

The child's face contorted. "No! This is ours. This was our deal!"

At that, my eyes snapped open. "This was not the deal. I wanted to live here with my family. That was all I wanted. Not this. Never this."

Rattling metal rang hollow within the silo. Screeching as the tremors forced it to shed its rust. A panel of siding slipped free and clanged to the ground. The silo was collapsing.

I needed to get him out of here before it fell in on us. Christian wouldn't leave unless I went with him, so I stood and pulled us toward the door.

"This was what you wanted!" The child screamed.

That was true a long time ago. Back when the kids at school teased me and I wanted to be anywhere other than at home. The child in front of me was angry and desperate for security, but I'm an adult now. I decided what was safe for my family and this was not safe for Christian.

"No," I said. "It's what you wanted. We're not the same person. Not anymore."

Taking the hint, Christian ushered me out of the dilapidated building, covering my head with his arm as we made a break for it. The building cried out with buckling aluminum and busting screws, but it held out just long enough for us to get through the door and into the night.

The Silo fell in on itself in a reluctant manner, like an earthquake rolling along the hillside, the ground rumbled with aftershocks. There was a final groan of protest before the top fell, tearing the sidewall like a banana peel all the way down to the base.

"Let's get out of here before someone calls the police," Christian urged.

Giving one last look at the heap, I took his hand with my good arm and went back to the house. This was the right decision. I couldn't believe that I'd even consider staying here and leaving him behind. It was like a trance of some kind, pulling me down, urging me to release the air from my lungs and inhale death.

If I had stayed, the silo would've fallen on me and killed me. Christian might've died as well. That was one thing I'd never allow. Even in my worst moments, I'd never let any harm come to him.

I'd face the Miles family and tell them the truth. They could hate me or forgive me, it didn't matter just so long as they knew they were safe. Though, I'd rather break my other arm than tell them that I was the problem. No, I wouldn't create new ghosts by withholding a truth they deserved to know.

Squeezing Christian's hand, the fear subsided. If he could love me after all of this, then nothing else mattered. We made it to the car and the air felt different. Plain and ordinary, if not a little skunky. It seemed the animals on the property were offended by the commotion.

He opened the car door to help me in, and that's when I saw it.

"Christian, look."

The porch light had finally given out.

28

---·---

AFTERSHOCKS

"Are you ready?"

Hell yes, I was ready. Giving the doctor the signal, he turned on the handheld saw. It whined and zipped as tiny blades sliced through the cast. A plume of white dust and debris created its own tiny atmosphere around my arm before he switched the thing off. Jiggling the cast loose, the air hit my skin for the first time in five months. My arm was exposed, and it was not pretty.

Dead hair and congealed dead skin caked in layers. It smelled like a ball sack. I made a sound of disgust and had to turn away. Christian, for whatever reason, found the whole process intriguing.

He was inches away from the flake field. "It's so... skinny."

"She wasn't using this arm," the doctor explained. "A little loss in muscle isn't uncommon."

"It's not like I was much to begin with."

"In a few weeks it will be like nothing happened."

If only that were true in all aspects of our life. After Robert left the hospital, he stayed on with us while he packed the family's belongings and prepared to move. What was estimated as a few weeks lingered into months, but when he asked us lunch, we assumed he had news.

"Think he's finally got his shit together?" I asked.

Christian shrugged. "Either that or Amy is going to drive down here and do it for him."

He pushed open the doors for me even though both arms were now free. I just smiled and walked through. We met Robert in an Applebee's bar where he waited with a Bud Light, his eyes fixed on the basketball game.

"Hey man," Christian greeted as we joined him.

Robert had a few new scars. That was to be expected after the ordeal he went through. I was surprised Amy didn't come running when the hospital called. She must've been too angry with him. Even if I was furious with Christian, I'd never leave him in a hospital alone.

"So, I don't want to keep you," he started. "I know you're busy. I just wanted to let you know that I received an offer on the farm."

Both men were eyeing me.

I hesitated when they did. "A new family or..."

At that, Robert's Adam's apple bobbed in his throat. "With the silo gone, the value of the property tripled. A couple of investors want to build condominiums there."

I frowned at that. Not because the farm would be demolished — we were well past that — but because it just seemed out of place. "Well, as long as you got paid."

He grinned, indicating he had. "Amy is happy. It's enough to get me out of the doghouse. Paul is happier in Colorado anyhow. He plans on going to State."

"I've been trying to call her, she hasn't responded to me at all," I said.

I had tried calling her nine times over the last few months. She never called or texted me back. Bringing it up was probably asking for trouble, but I had to know. What had I done that made her shut me out? I mean, apart from haunting their house and driving them out of state.

I had every intention of telling them, but Christian talked me out of it. "Sometimes it's just better to leave things alone."

"Secrets are what got me into this mess in the first place," I argued.

"Yeah," he said slowly. "But I don't think they want to know. The haunting has been resolved. They moved away. They don't want to know, otherwise they'd ask."

Not only had Amy not asked, but she also never spoke to me again. It was like she knew it was me or blamed me. Either way, she wasn't wrong. After everything we went through with the Miles family, her silence lessened my regret. It was a shitty response, but lately I found myself shedding guilt the way a snake sheds its skin. I left it and moved on, no more carrying it around with me.

Robert nodded and took a sip of his beer as if he were trying to find the best way to frame his response. "Amy just wants to start over. Pretend none of this ever happened."

She wanted to pretend I never happened.

As someone who struggled with female friends, it felt like high school all over again. The other girls noticed me and took their herd elsewhere. Still, I couldn't blame her for wanting to pretend this blip in her life never existed. We all have our coping mechanisms.

"I don't think her heart was ever here," I said. "She missed home."

"I wish you guys had a better experience in Washington," Christian said. "It's a beautiful place when it's not haunted."

"Well, with Paul wanting to go to college in Colorado and Amy's family there, it just makes sense. I jumped on what I thought was an opportunity and it bit me in the ass. I wasn't thinking when I bought that place."

My brows raised, giving me away. It never occurred to me that Robert had bought the place sight unseen without discussing it with his family first. I glanced at Christian, and he was also just as perplexed by that information.

I was beginning to realize that maybe there was a reason it took Robert Miles months to move back to Colorado. Why his family was so unhappy with him. None of it had to do with me.

"Well, if you're making money, I'm happy for you," I said. "Really. I want the best for your family."

"Charity doesn't seem to remember anything. Lacy might, but she's a tough little thing."

Small mercies well deserved.

"So, I take it this is your two weeks?" Christian said with a clap of his hands.

"Ah, about that," Robert said. "I'm actually leaving tonight."

We were right about the purpose of his invitation at least. My stomach tremored at the thought of scrambling for a new hire. Labor Ready always had men on the sidelines, but sometimes they didn't show up. Never knew what kind of person we'd get until they were on the site holding a piece of rebar like it was a grenade.

"We'll work it out," Christian assured me. "One of the guys we just took on is working out. We can offer him a full-time position."

And just like that, our family shrank to just Christian and I. That night, when we went to bed, I couldn't help but think about the worst.

What if something happened to him? Would I lose control and subconsciously drag others down with me? End up creating a whole new nexus event designed to punish those I blamed or force people to remain with me.

After the events on the property, I'd try to make things happen, but they never did. The lights didn't flicker and there was no porch light in my dreams. Nothing. Not a single surge of power or dark subconscious thoughts trickling into my psyche.

Whatever gave me that ability must've been conditional. Not something I could do on my own. But what?

It was me as a child that we found in the silo. Apart from having my whole life uprooted when I was seven, what else happened at that time? Grandpa died. The first few months of living with Mom was a chaotic ride. She decided to leave one of her boyfriends in the night. Scooping me up, she carried me to the van, and we drove away without looking back.

Even as a small child, I didn't question what we were doing. Leaving that awful guy who walked around the house in his underwear. His house was boring and sometimes, I would wake up screaming.

No — wait — I never *woke up* screaming. I was already awake. Mom kept insisting that I was having a nightmare, so I must've convinced myself that was the case. My eyes went wide as I clutched the sheets. How could I forget such a thing?

The talons wrapped around the aluminum frame of my window. A voice so wrong, like a thousand maggots feasting on roadkill.

I kept my window closed at night. Locked, even. Despite being on the second story with no way to climb up, it always found a way inside. I clamped a hand over my mouth so Christian wouldn't hear the soft whine seeping from my mouth.

It spoke to me, that thing obscured by the shadows. The moonlight defused along its fur. No larger than a racoon, but there were no cute ear tufts or chittering undulations. Talons the size of, I don't know, a big fucking bird. What kind of bird had fur? I don't think it even had wings, but it reminded me of a massive owl. I never could see the face.

"Why do you cry?" It spoke with a melody of an old woman recalling an ancient song. Harsh with age and knowledge.

Mom said it was a nightmare, and what else could it be? She said I had been through a rough time, and I was struggling to cope. She was right on that count, so why couldn't the other be true as well?

"Why do you cry?"

I didn't speak it out loud, but when prompted, all my child fears and desires reeled through my mind. I wanted to go back home and live with my grandparents. Even if it was impossible. As if the creature could read my thoughts, it cooed in response.

In a fit of terror, I reached for the nearest thing—a Dumbo plushy—and chucked it at the thing. The creature was thrown off balance and disappeared from the window. It didn't fly away like a bird, it just slid back and fell. Slamming the window shut, I returned to my bed and rocked with my knees tucked under my chin.

Once the shock subsided, I screamed for Mom, only to have her boyfriend respond.

"Shut up!"

So, I did. I never spoke another word about the thing in the window and forced myself to believe it was a dream. Even if I never found Dumbo. It was a nightmare. I must've just imagined I had that plushy. There were so many on my bed, and we left them all behind the night we fled from that house anyway.

The tears were rolling into my hair as I bit my knuckles. The irony wasn't lost on me. I haunted people with memories that didn't belong to me because I refused to acknowledge my memory of the creature, and the deal we must've made that night.

Shortly after that was when Grandma learned that the silo couldn't be torn down. The new owner was furious and wanted to sue her for withholding relevant information, but it wasn't like they could prove anything. When the surveyors came and noted the rare, endangered owls in the silo, it was news to everyone including Grandma.

A new fear struck me then.

"This is what you wanted…" the child said. In the creature's mind, it upheld its side of the bargain. Did I uphold mine? Did I make an offering I didn't understand? I was a child with nothing to offer, too terrified to speak let alone agree to sell my soul.

When the sun rose, I was still staring at the ceiling. But when the alarm went off, so did my worries. Christian kissed me on the forehead while I pretended to sleep before getting ready for work. A warm, fuzzy feeling came over me then. I had no idea he did that.

It's hard to be worried about things you can't understand.

Like the silo and the farm, the past was being demolished and paved for new life. I couldn't live waiting for the day a monster may or may not come to collect. It wanted me to stay in the crumbling silo to die but I didn't. My dream did not come true, yet I survived.

I only hoped that was the case for its next victim too.

— • —

EPILOGUE

F lat as far as the horizon, the property had been a vacant plot of land, untouched and ideal for building. Graham was full of plots like this one. Twenty minutes from downtown and a quarter mile from the neighbor's custom-built home. Not unlike the one we planned to build.

The man with the clipboard came back with the soil sample I'd been wringing my hands over for the last week.

"Everything is good to go," he said, adjusting his hardhat.

It was more than a little silly that he had to wear one here, there wasn't a single tree. There were a ton of blackberry bushes and weeds, but nothing that could fall on him. Either by policy or habit, that hardhat remained despite the summer heat.

I silently cheered the fact that the land wasn't swampland, contaminated, or otherwise unsuitable for building on. All of those things were unlikely, but it didn't mean I wouldn't fret all the same. Christian and I had been working for two years to get to this point, and the last thing we needed was another hitch in the plans.

Pulling me in, Christian smiled. I was grinning ear to ear.

Once the septic system was in place, he could lay the foundation and get started on our first home.

Given that nearly half of his jobs were in this area, it just made sense to move. There was no reason to remain so close to Seattle when he worked the occasional odd job out there every few months while I worked at home.

When our lease ended, the complex increased our rent by an additional three hundred dollars, prompting the discussion of building our own house.

"At this rate, a mortgage would be cheaper," one of us would say.

We had been stashing money away for the last two years for the right time, but when it came, it wasn't a joyful move. Our savings was intended for a downpayment, but it was also for slow winter seasons, accidents, or anything that might go wrong. All those things could still happen, but we'd be eighty grand short if they did.

Christian says that worrying is my favorite pastime. He's probably right.

After visiting a few open houses, it became clear that building a home was the only option for us. Between my apprehension of neighborhoods, hauntings, former owners paying a visit, and Christian's scrupulous eye, nothing felt right.

After an unsettling visit to a home with countless pieces of clear tape stuck to a wall like they once held up pictures of things I did not want to see, Christian made some calls and hired a buddy to draw up a blueprint.

Nothing too large or extravagant. A basic starter home that could be built on in later years if we needed to. A few bedrooms, bathrooms, and a larger kitchen as I decided it was time to learn how to cook like a decent human being. We couldn't live on sandwiches forever.

"This is it?" he asked me.

It better be. I spent far too much time and energy on this patch of land. No backing out now. I squinted against the daylight and nodded. "We're going to need a nice outdoor space."

"Of course."

"Some trees..." We would need a lot of trees. This property was barren, but in a good way. We could shape and mold it into the dream we shared.

"Sure, why not?"

"One of those tall, iron fences like the neighbors have."

Christian let out a sigh. "What have I gotten myself into?"

"Just a lifetime of work and a never-ending job," I teased.

"What about a dog?" Christian asked.

I hesitated at that. A dog is a lot of responsibility. I'd be the one to train it and take care of it while he got to be the fun parent. Still, it might motivate him to get the fence done sooner. "We'll look into it once the fence is up," I said. "A scrappy mut?"

"What about those giant fluffy dogs?" he asked. "The kind in those videos that sleep with chickens and goats jump around on them?"

We wouldn't need a security system if we got what he was thinking of. "A Great Pyrenees?"

"Yeah, the great pair of knees."

Gail would love to know we planned on getting a dog. She had finally come to terms with the fact that we didn't plan on having kids. We never did speak about the farm. I think everyone was so tired of hearing me talk about it—I was tired of hearing me talk about it.

It's so funny the way people compartmentalize events that take a departure from their reality. I only brought it up once as an offer of closure.

"They're going to demolish the farm," I told her.

"About time!"

That would've upset me years prior, but these days I have too much to do and look forward to. "I know, I thought about parking across the street with popcorn, but I'm up to my ass in paperwork."

"But still no kids?" Gail asked.

I shook my head even though the conversation was over the phone. I hated it when she asked that. We were a complete family as we were. But I supposed a dog would be a kind of compromise. Gail would have to knit really big sweaters if we got the kind of dog Christian wanted.

I'd need to do some research. A lot of research, but they did seem very sweet and lazy. "I'll look into them. See if they need special training or something."

"Due diligence is required."

Always.